squish

POD VS. POD

BY JENNIFER L. HOLM & MATTHEW HOLM

RANDOM HOUSE NEW YORK

This is a work of fiction. Names, characters, places, and incidents either are the product of the authors' imagination or are used fictitiously. Any resemblance to actual persons, living or dead, events, or locales is entirely coincidental.

Published in the United States by Random House Children's Books, a division of Penguin Random House LLC, New York.

Random House and the colophon are registered trademarks of Penguin Random House LLC.

Visit us on the Web! randomhousekids.com

Educators and librarians, for a variety of teaching tools, visit us at RHTeachersLibrarians.com

Library of Congress Cataloging-in-Publication Data is available upon request.

ISBN 978-0-307-98308-4 (trade) —
ISBN 978-0-307-98309-1 (lib. bdg.) —
ISBN 978-0-307-98310-7 (ebook)

MANUFACTURED IN MALAYSIA 10 9 8 7 6 5 4 3
First Edition

Random House Children's Books supports the First Amendment and celebrates the right to read.

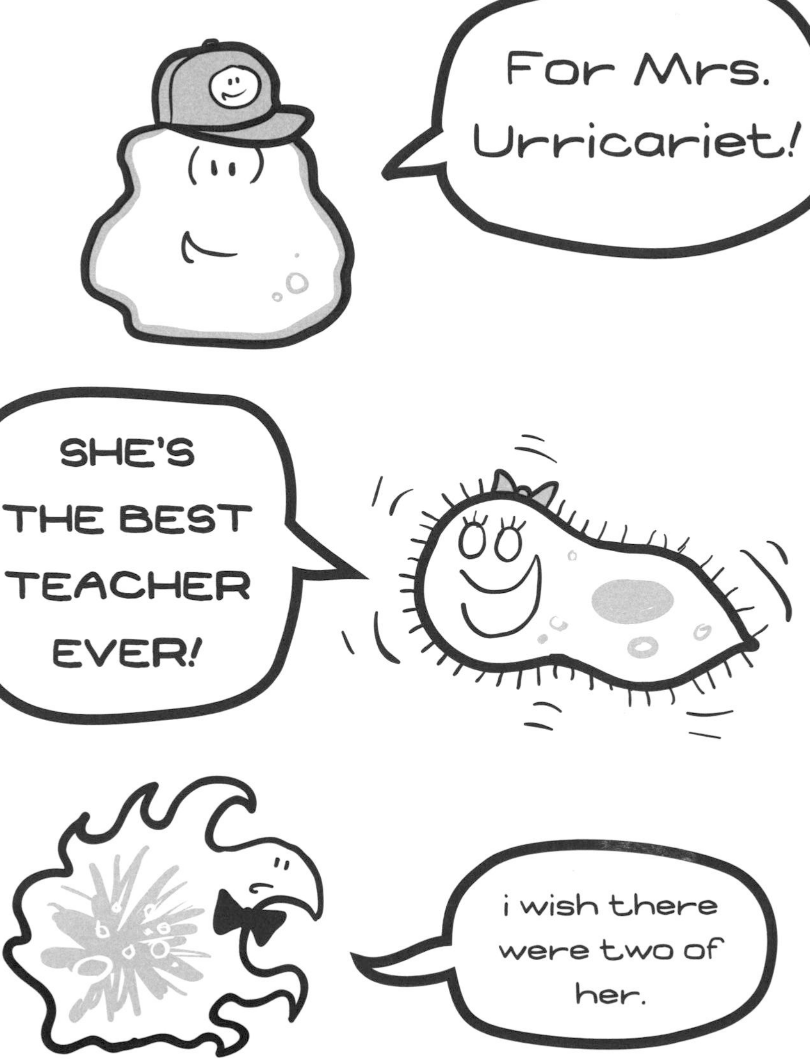

For Mrs. Urricariet!
SHE'S THE BEST TEACHER EVER!
i wish there were two of her.

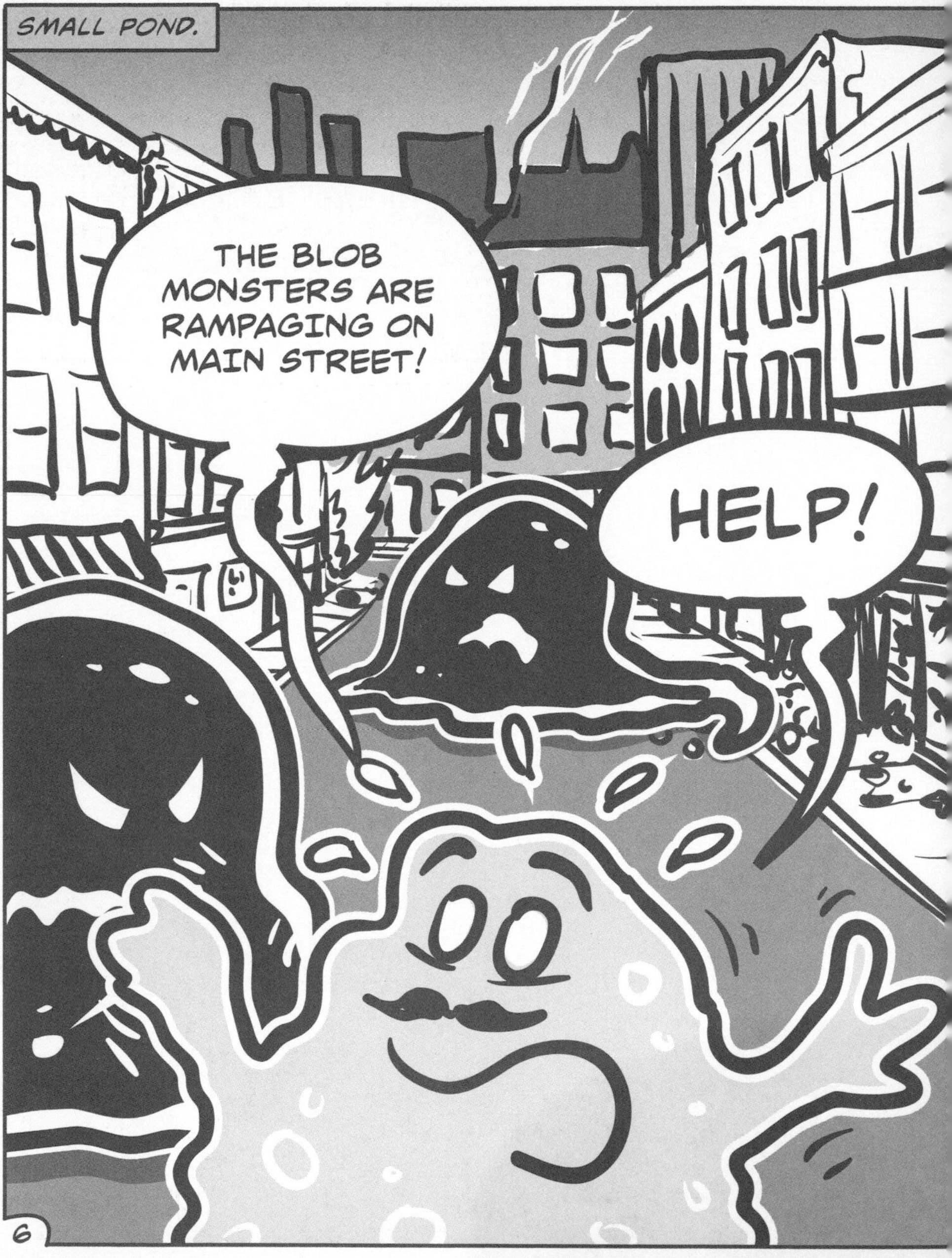
SMALL POND.
THE BLOB MONSTERS ARE RAMPAGING ON MAIN STREET!
HELP!

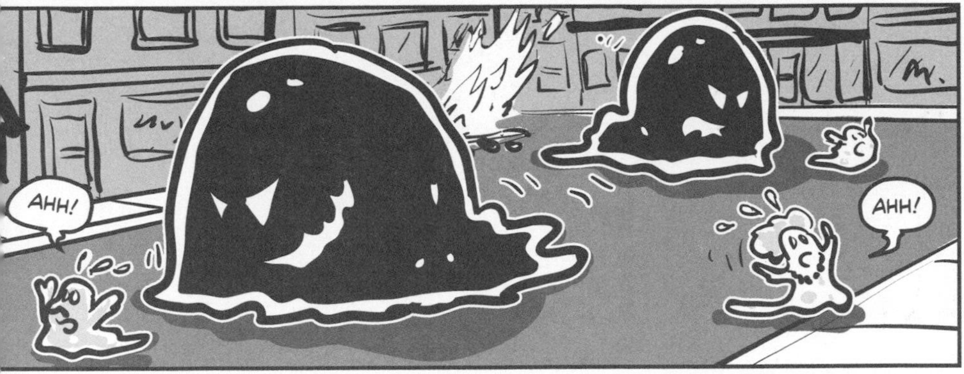
AHH!
AHH!

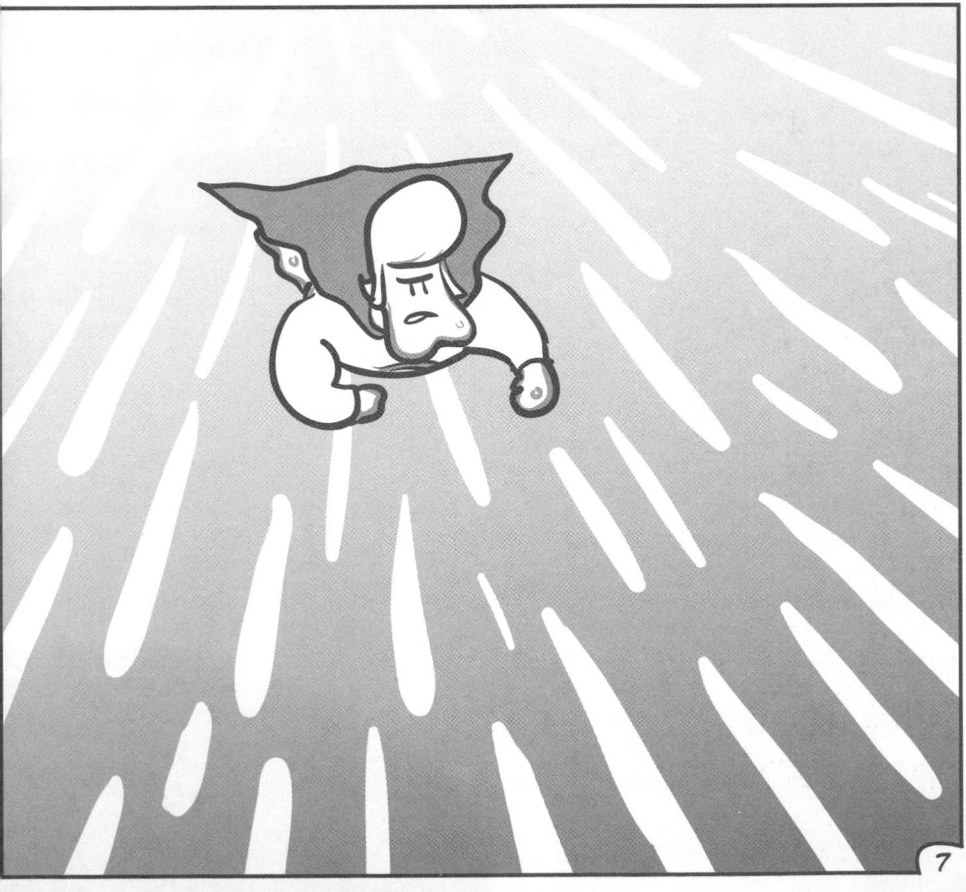

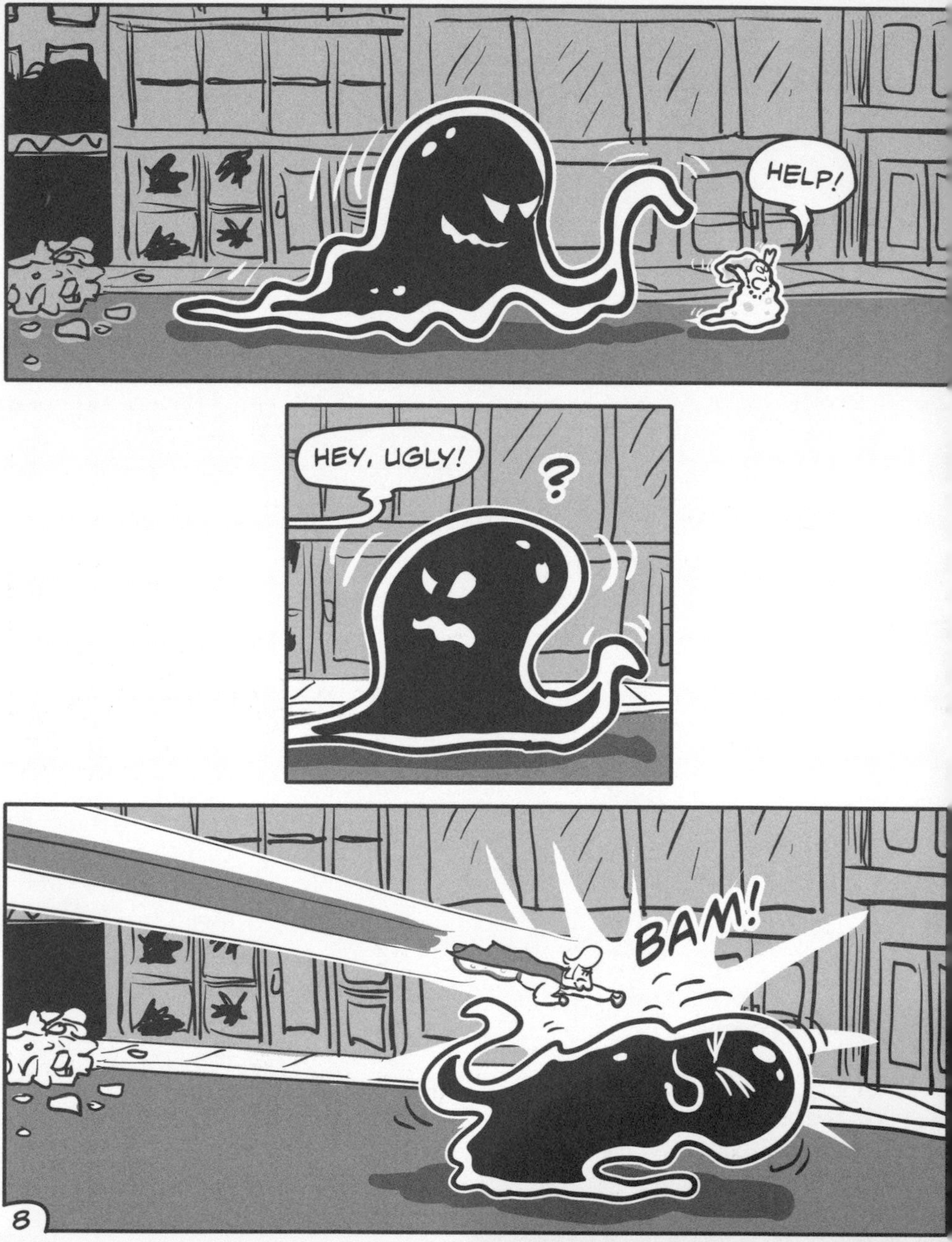
HELP!
HEY, UGLY!
?
BAM!

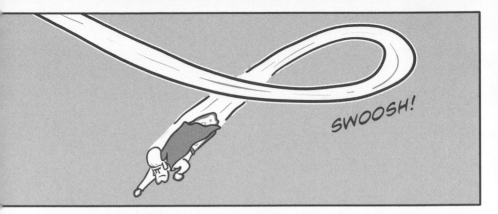

SWOOSH!

POW!

LEAP

WHAM!

9

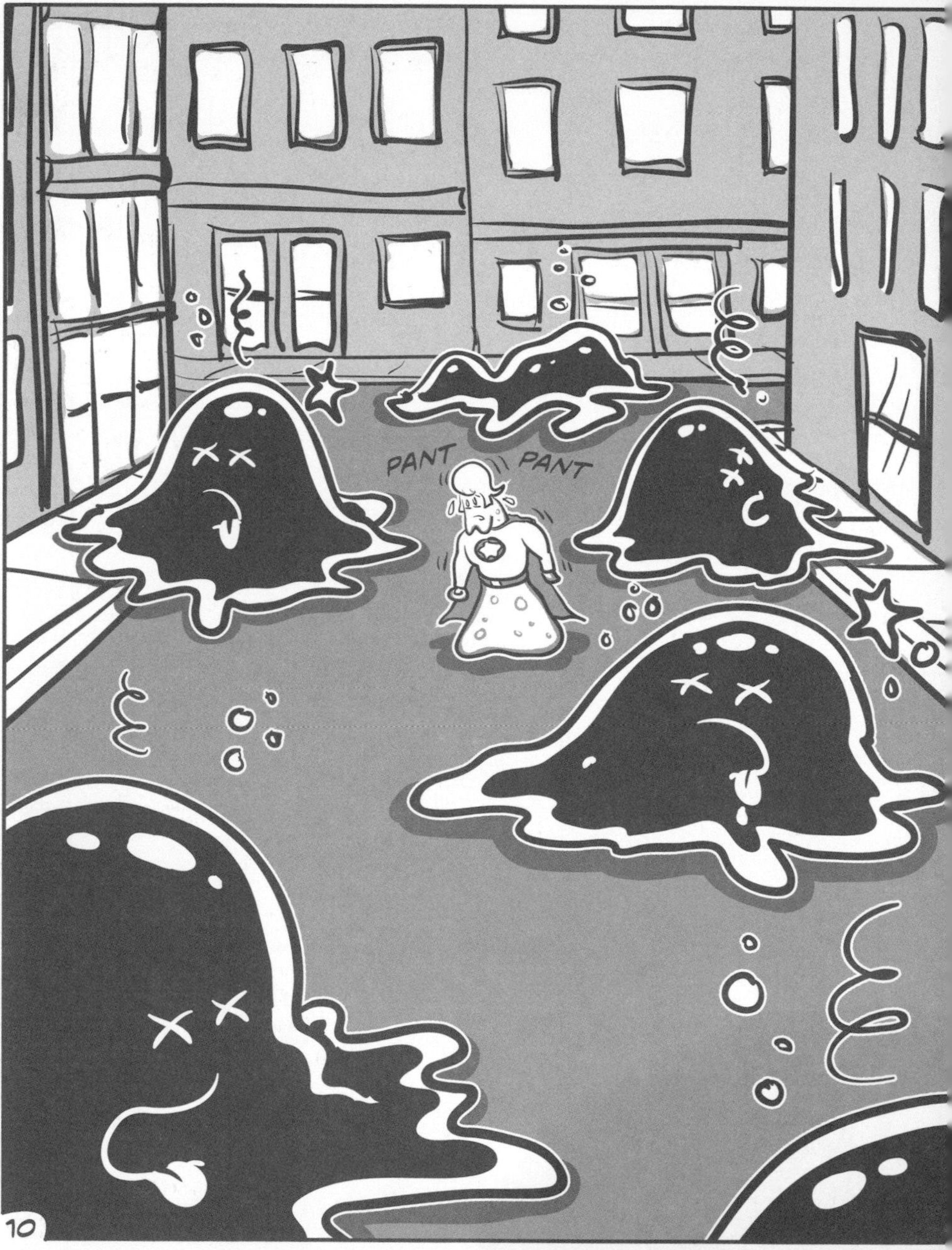
PANT PANT

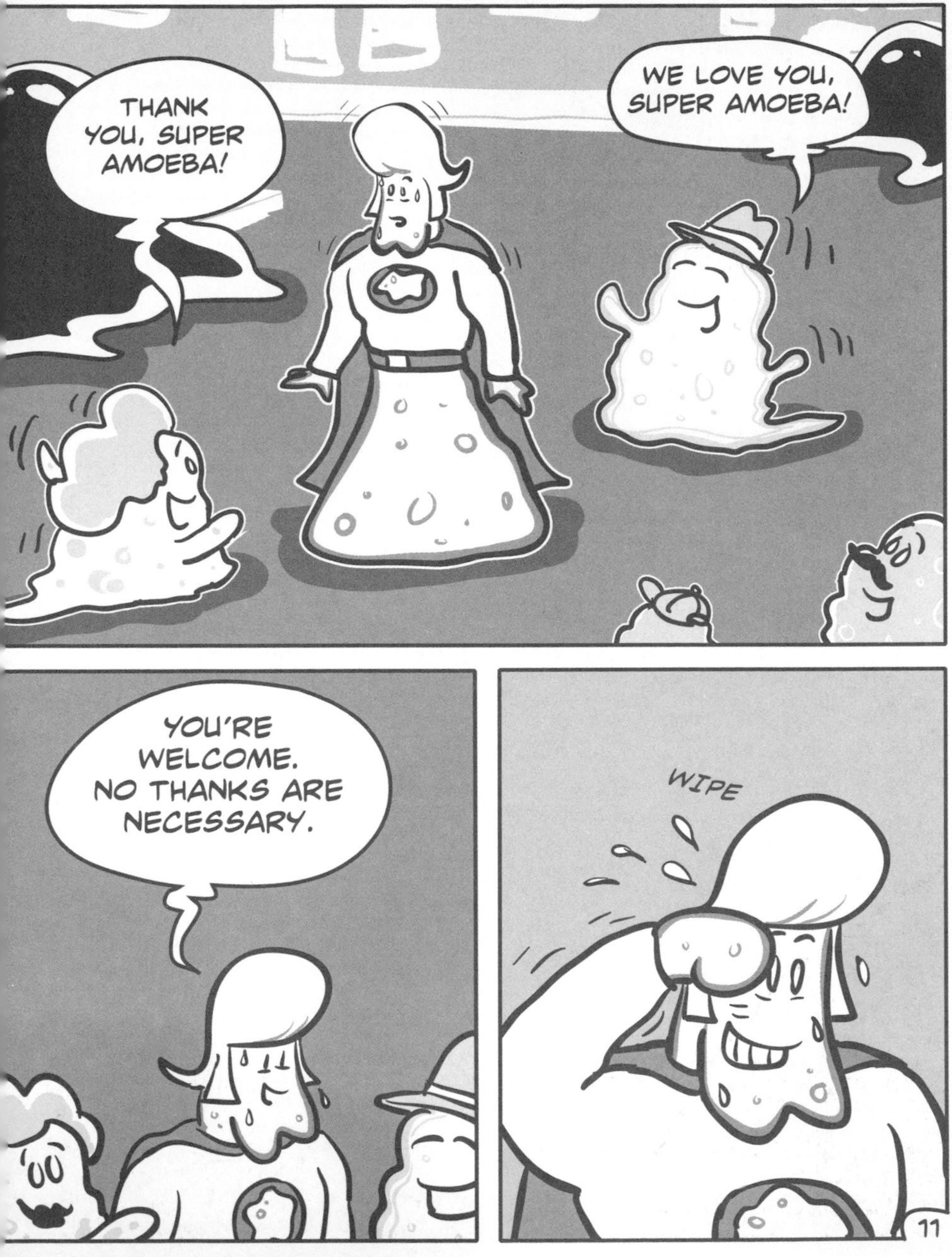
THANK YOU, SUPER AMOEBA!
WE LOVE YOU, SUPER AMOEBA!
YOU'RE WELCOME. NO THANKS ARE NECESSARY.
WIPE

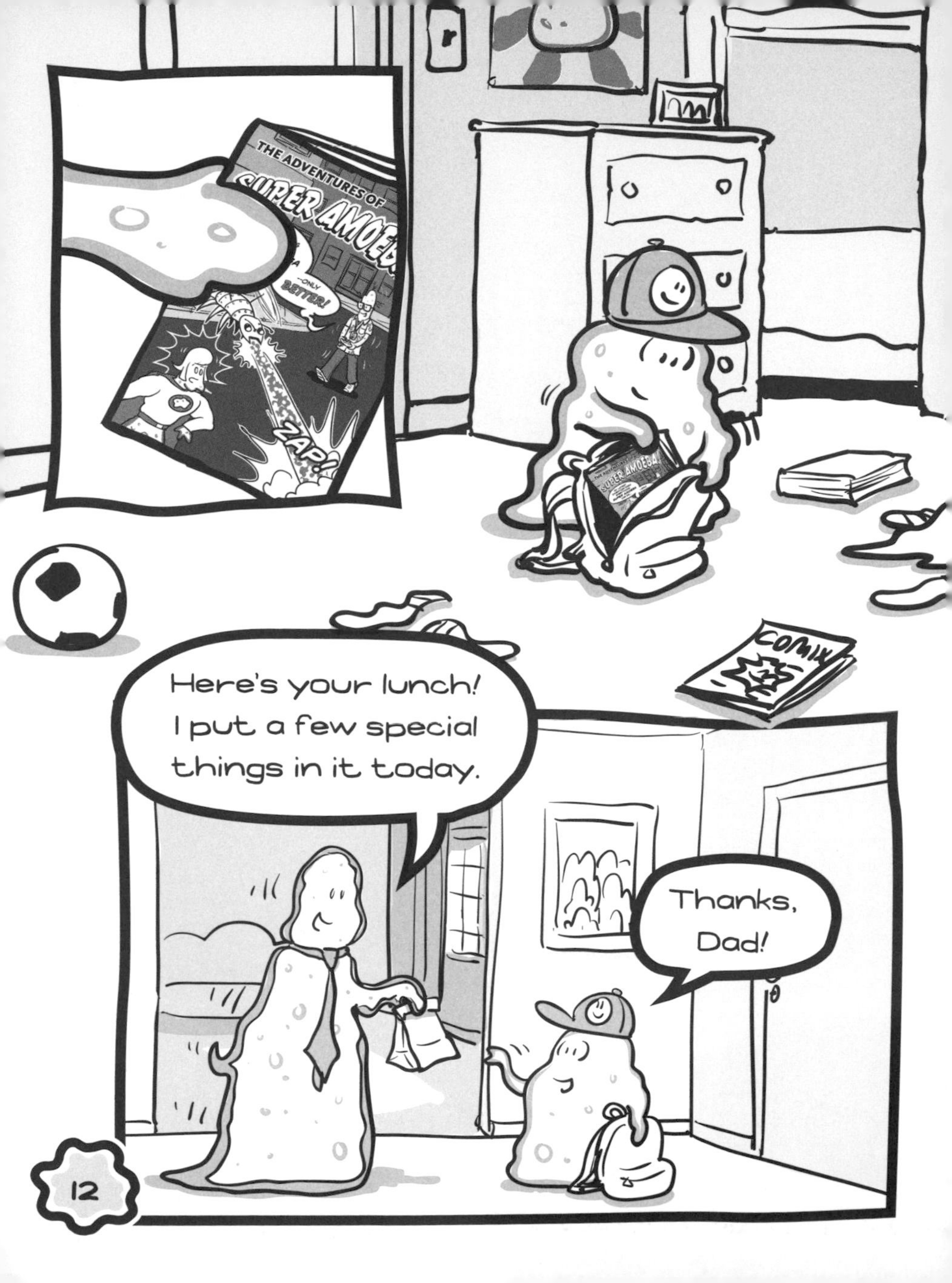
THE ADVENTURES OF
SUPER AMOEBA!
—ONLY
BETTER!
ZAP!
COMIX
Here's your lunch! I put a few special things in it today.
Thanks, Dad!

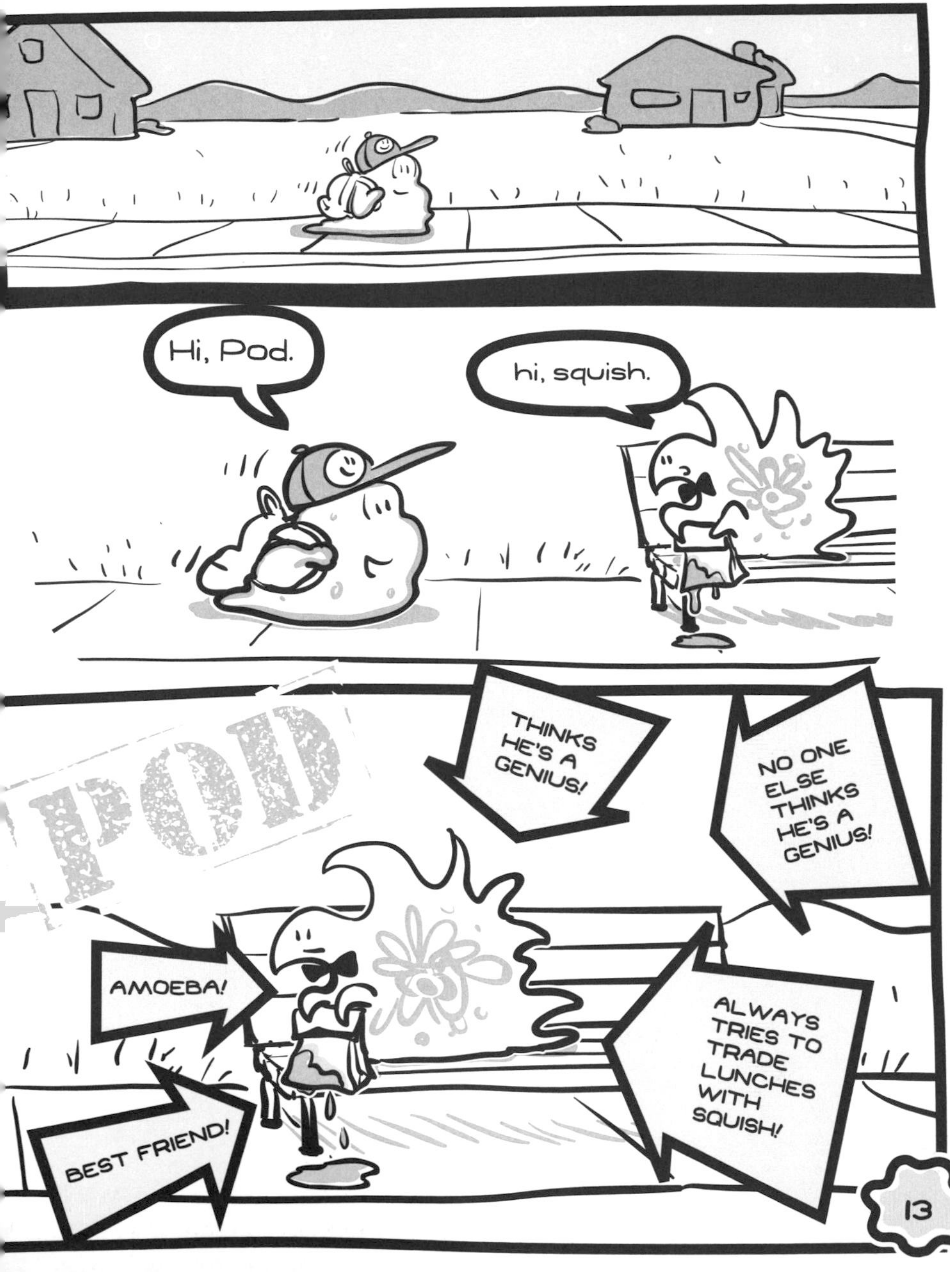
Hi, Pod.
hi, squish.
POD
THINKS HE'S A GENIUS!
NO ONE ELSE THINKS HE'S A GENIUS!
AMOEBA!
ALWAYS TRIES TO TRADE LUNCHES WITH SQUISH!
BEST FRIEND!

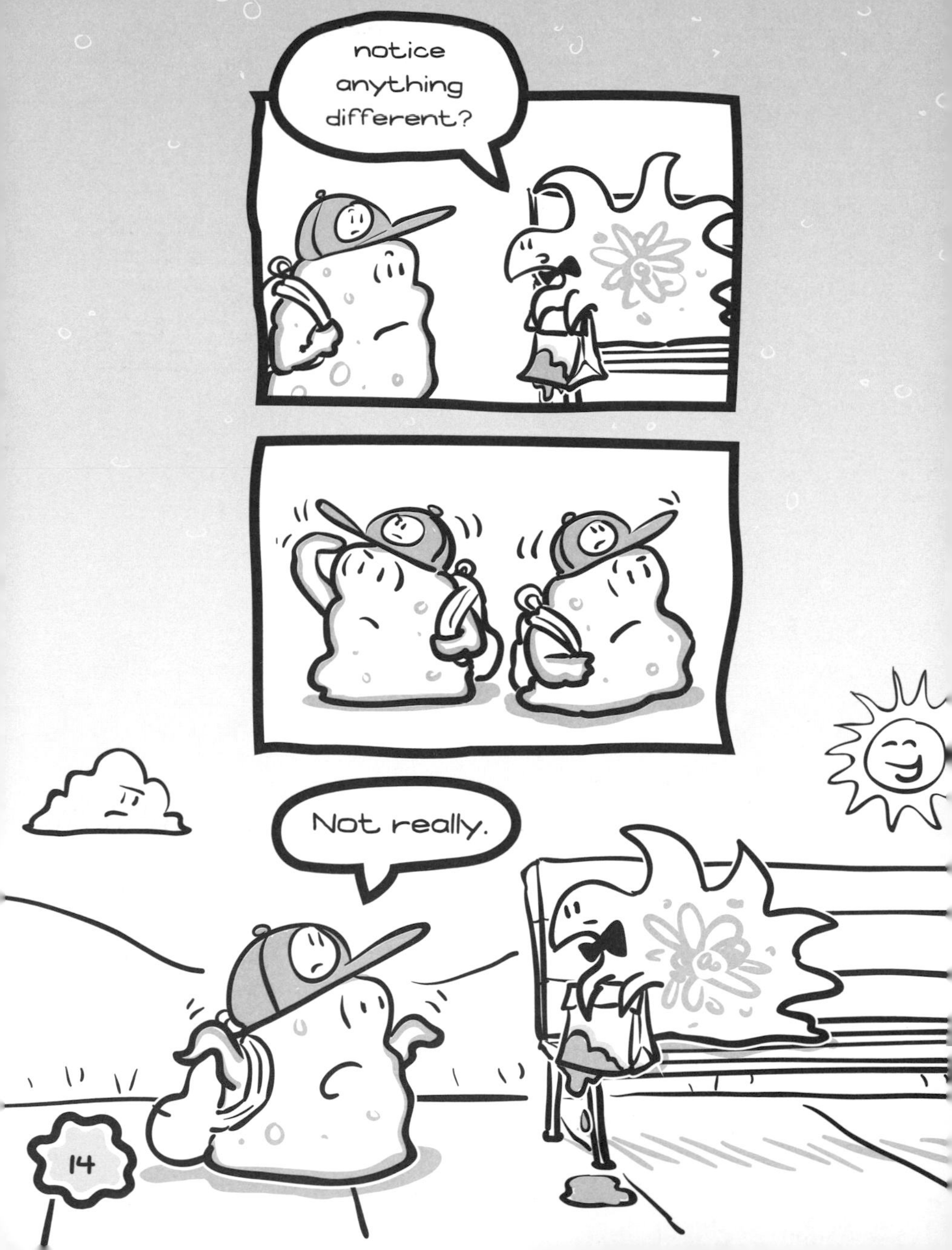
notice anything different?
Not really.

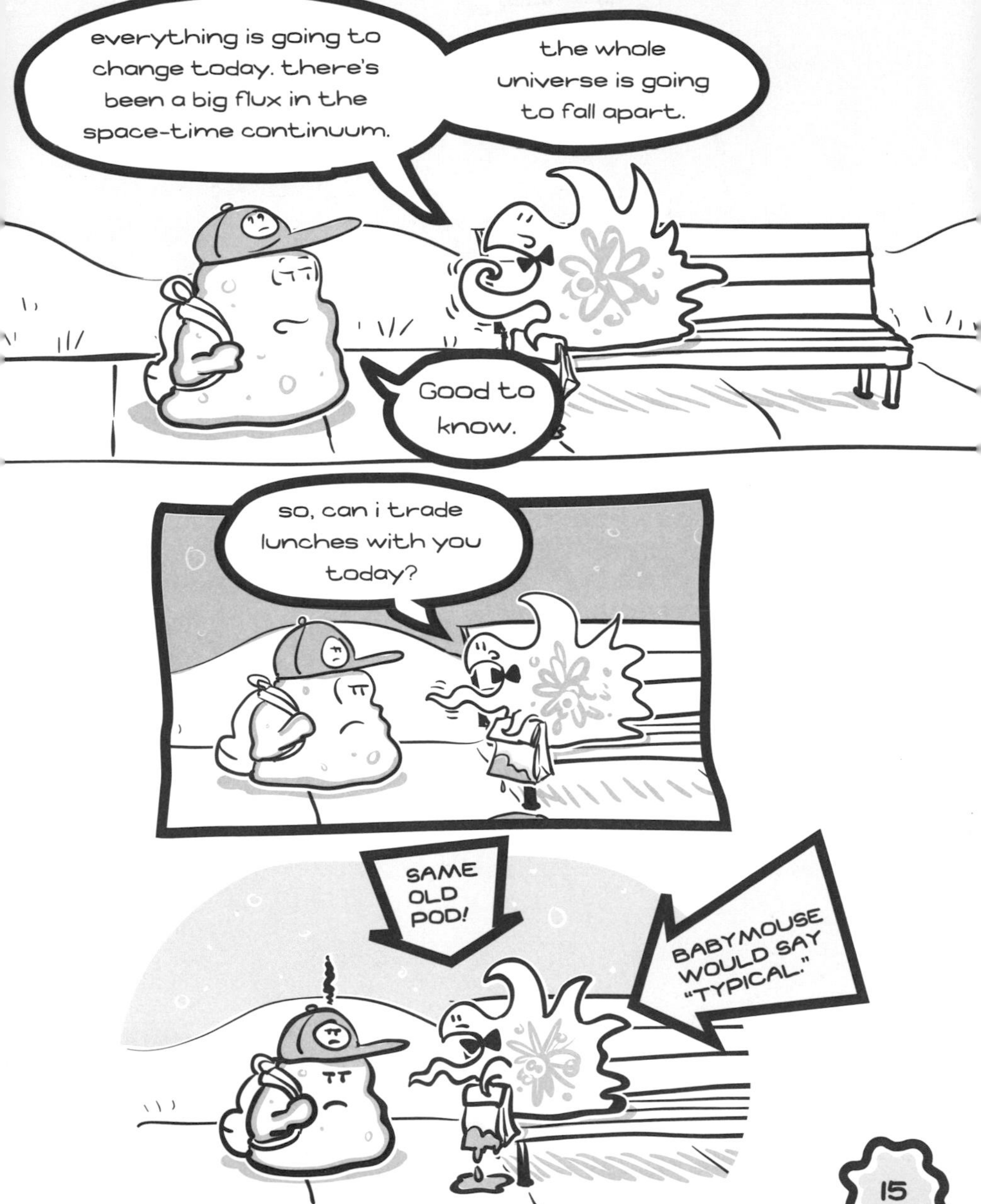
everything is going to change today. there's been a big flux in the space-time continuum.
the whole universe is going to fall apart.
Good to know.
so, can i trade lunches with you today?
SAME OLD POD!
BABYMOUSE WOULD SAY "TYPICAL."

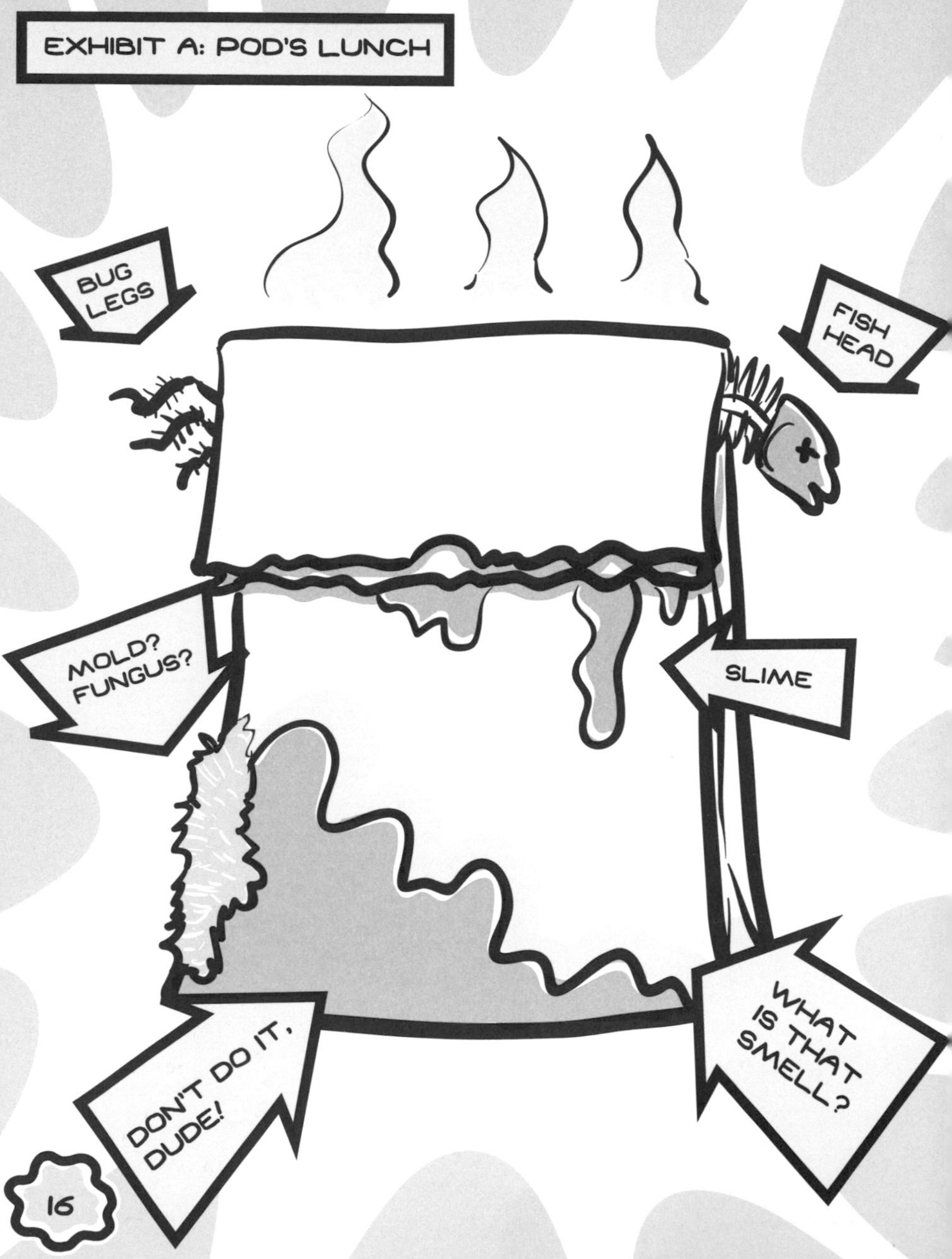
EXHIBIT A: POD'S LUNCH
BUG LEGS
FISH HEAD
MOLD? FUNGUS?
SLIME
DON'T DO IT, DUDE!
WHAT IS THAT SMELL?

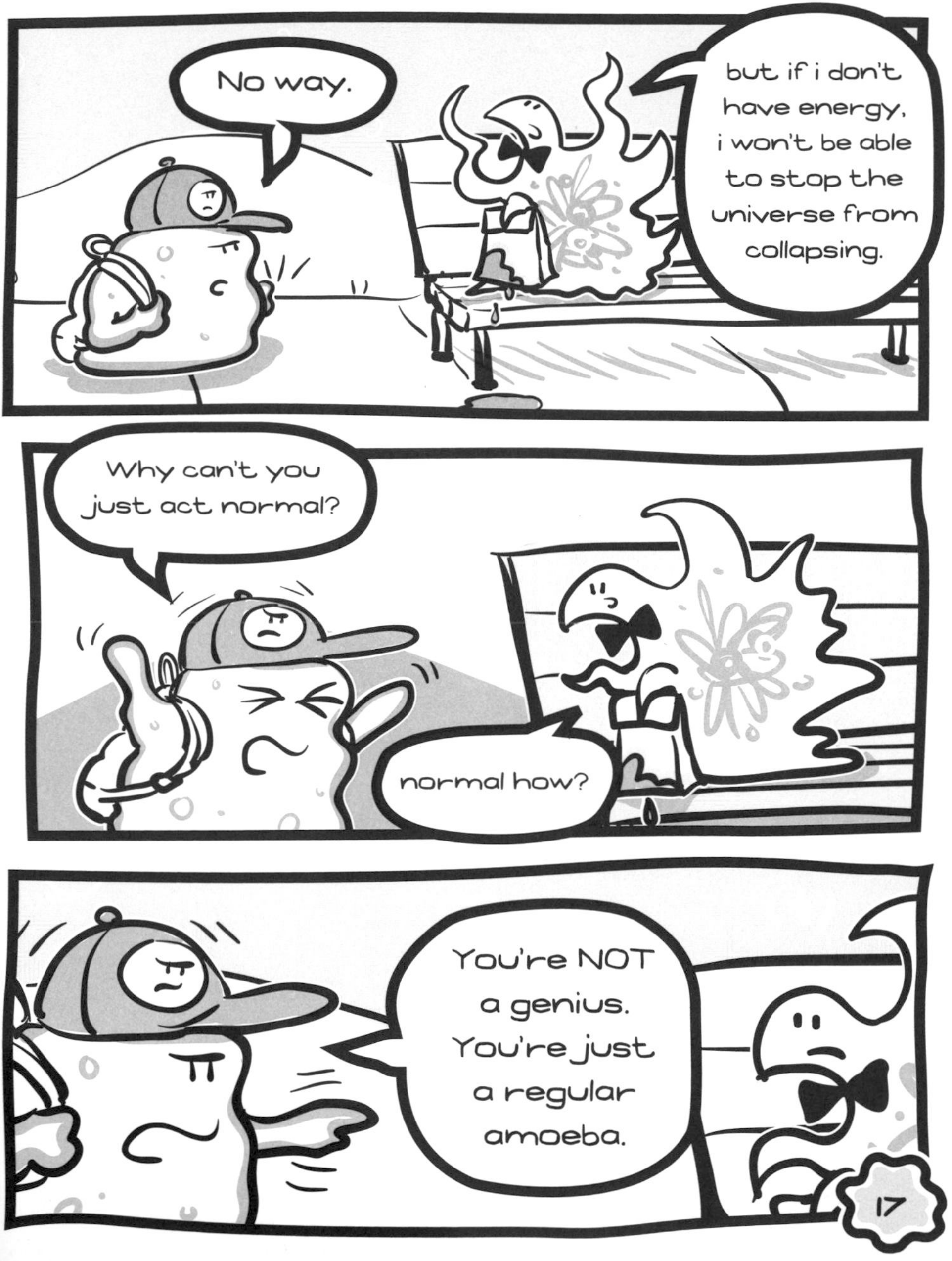
No way.
but if i don't have energy, i won't be able to stop the universe from collapsing.
Why can't you just act normal?
normal how?
You're NOT a genius. You're just a regular amoeba.
17

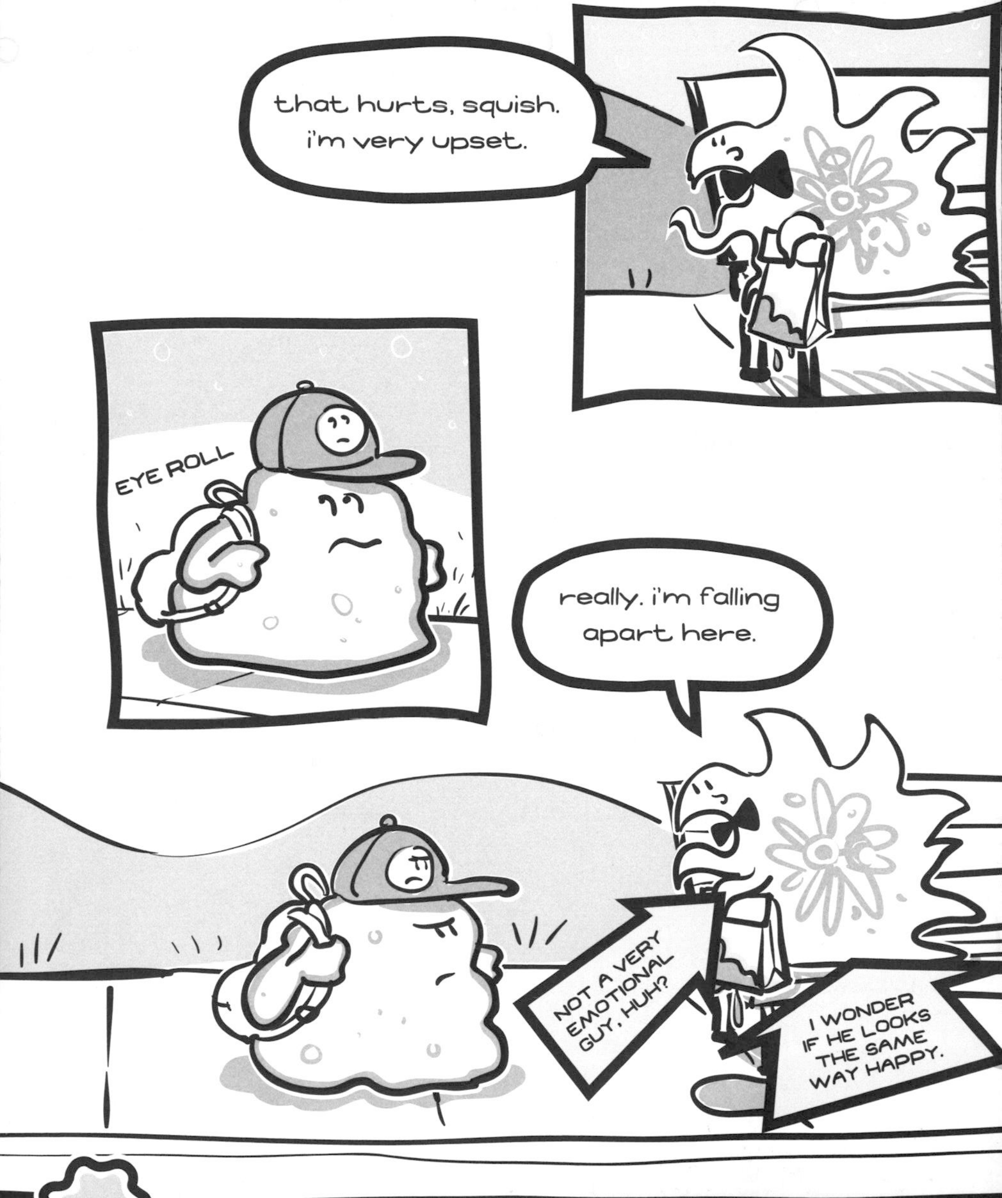
that hurts, squish.
i'm very upset.
EYE ROLL
really. i'm falling apart here.
NOT A VERY EMOTIONAL GUY, HUH?
I WONDER IF HE LOOKS THE SAME WAY HAPPY.

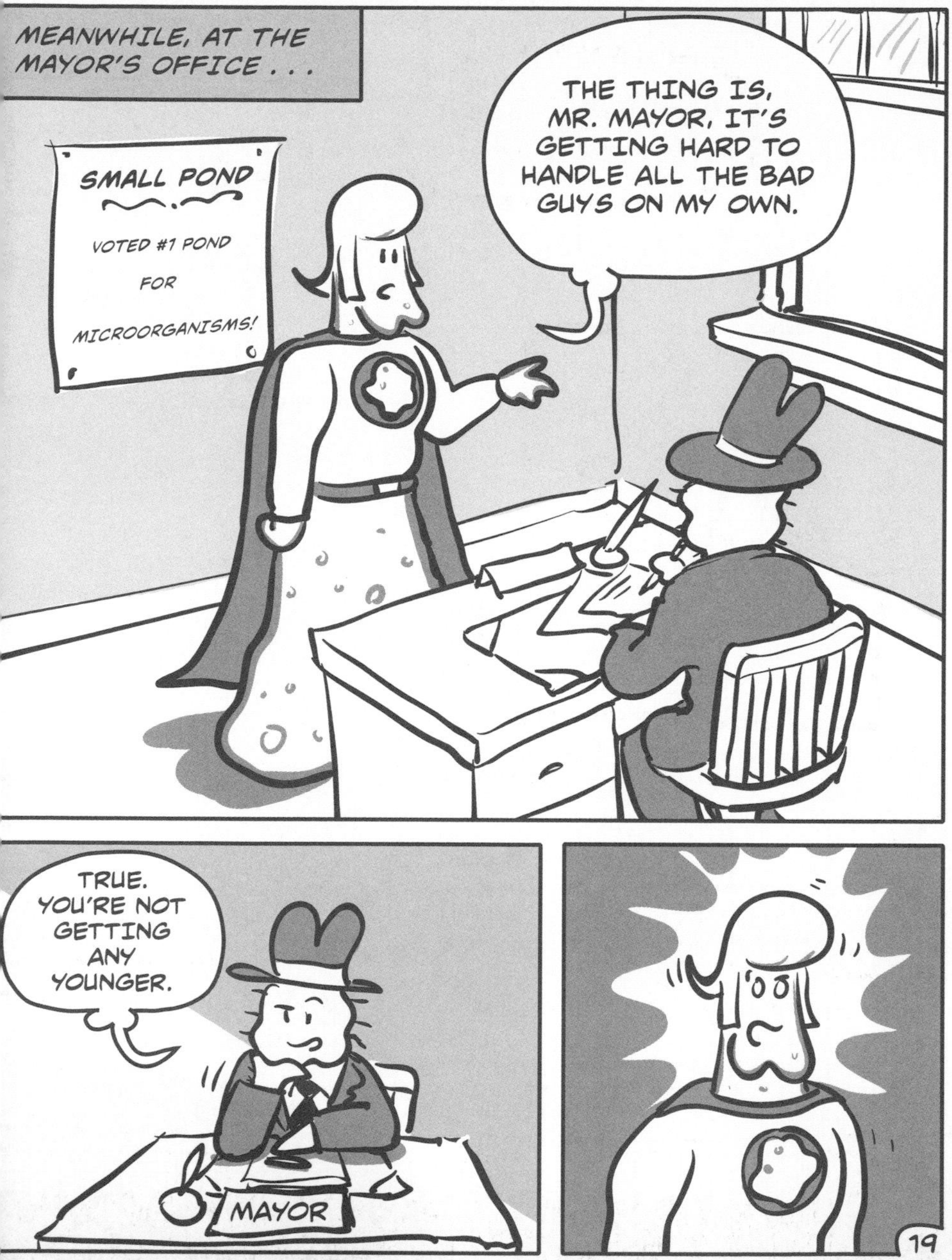
MEANWHILE, AT THE MAYOR'S OFFICE . . .
SMALL POND
VOTED #1 POND FOR MICROORGANISMS!
THE THING IS, MR. MAYOR, IT'S GETTING HARD TO HANDLE ALL THE BAD GUYS ON MY OWN.
TRUE. YOU'RE NOT GETTING ANY YOUNGER.
MAYOR

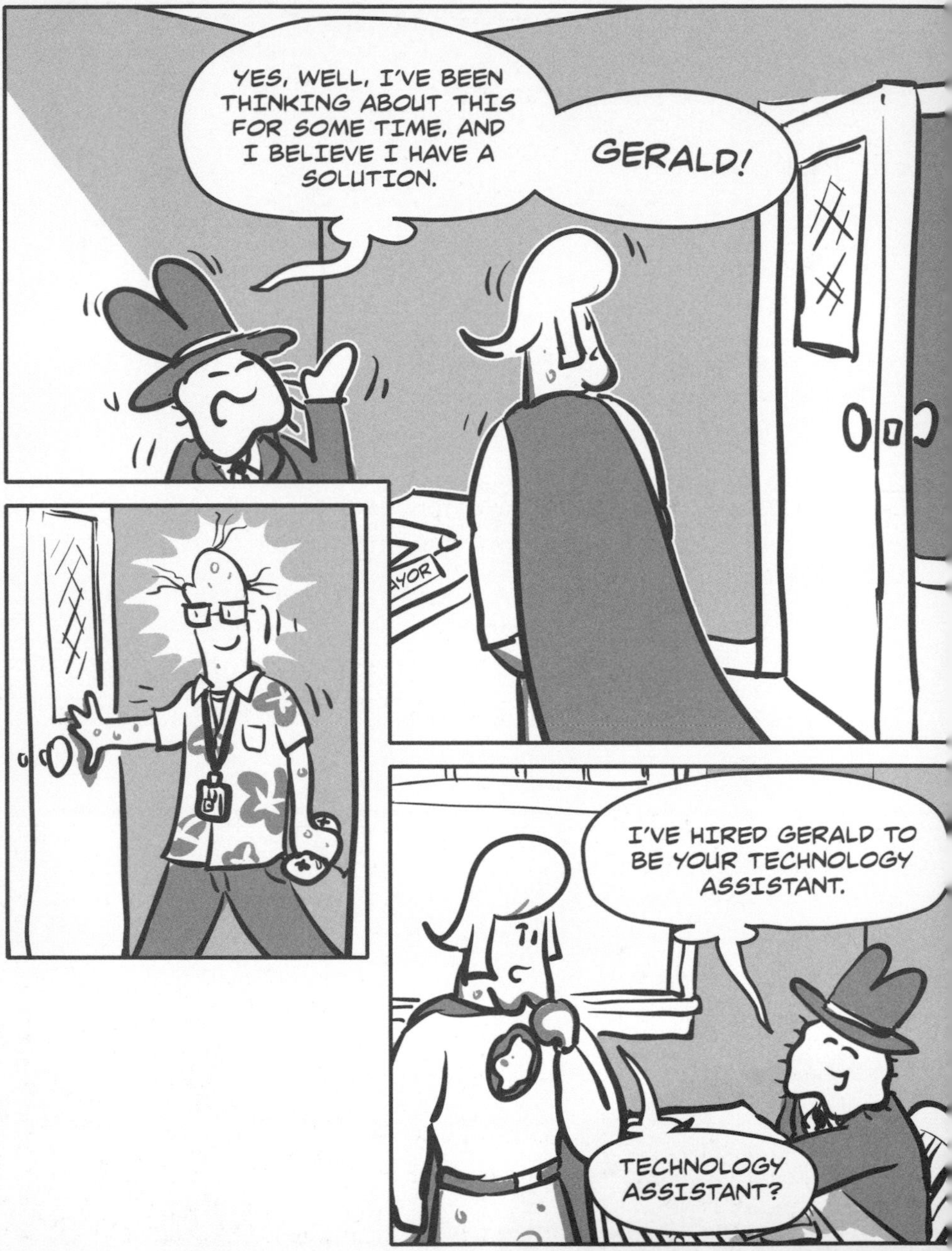
YES, WELL, I'VE BEEN THINKING ABOUT THIS FOR SOME TIME, AND I BELIEVE I HAVE A SOLUTION.
GERALD!
MAYOR
I'VE HIRED GERALD TO BE YOUR TECHNOLOGY ASSISTANT.
TECHNOLOGY ASSISTANT?

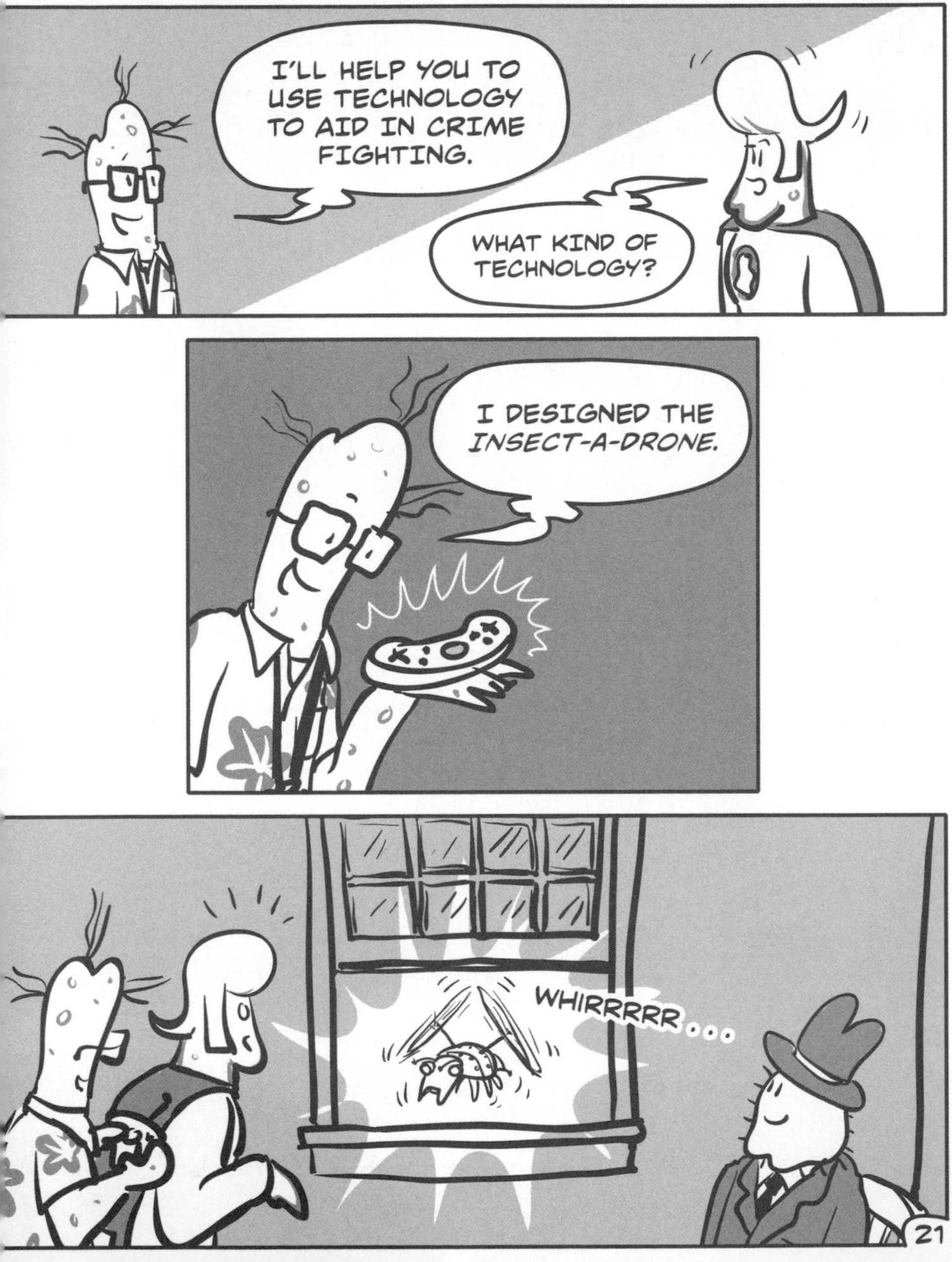
I'LL HELP YOU TO USE TECHNOLOGY TO AID IN CRIME FIGHTING.
WHAT KIND OF TECHNOLOGY?
I DESIGNED THE *INSECT-A-DRONE.*
WHIRRRRRR...

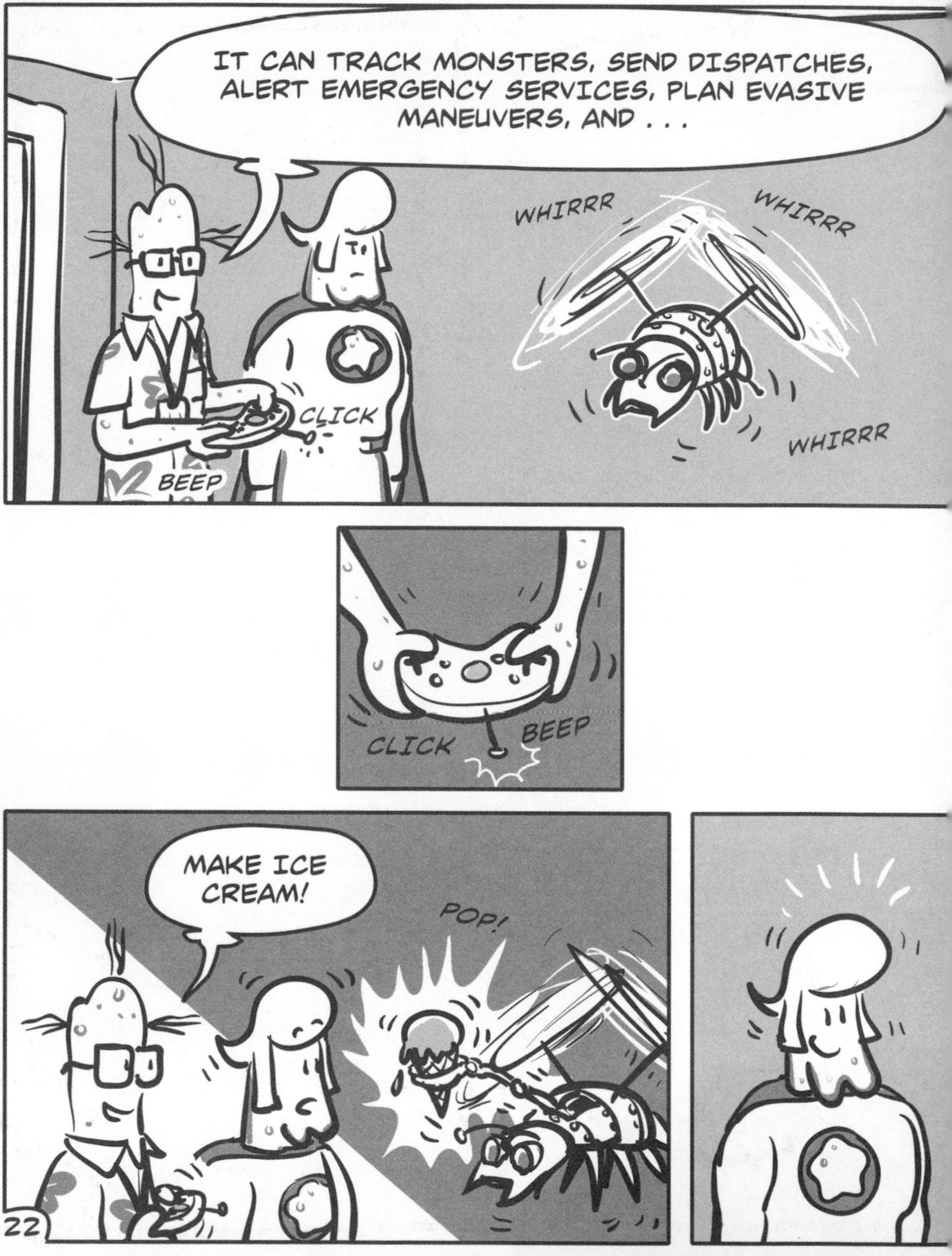
IT CAN TRACK MONSTERS, SEND DISPATCHES, ALERT EMERGENCY SERVICES, PLAN EVASIVE MANEUVERS, AND . . .
WHIRRR
WHIRRR
CLICK
BEEP
WHIRRR
CLICK
BEEP
MAKE ICE CREAM!
POP!

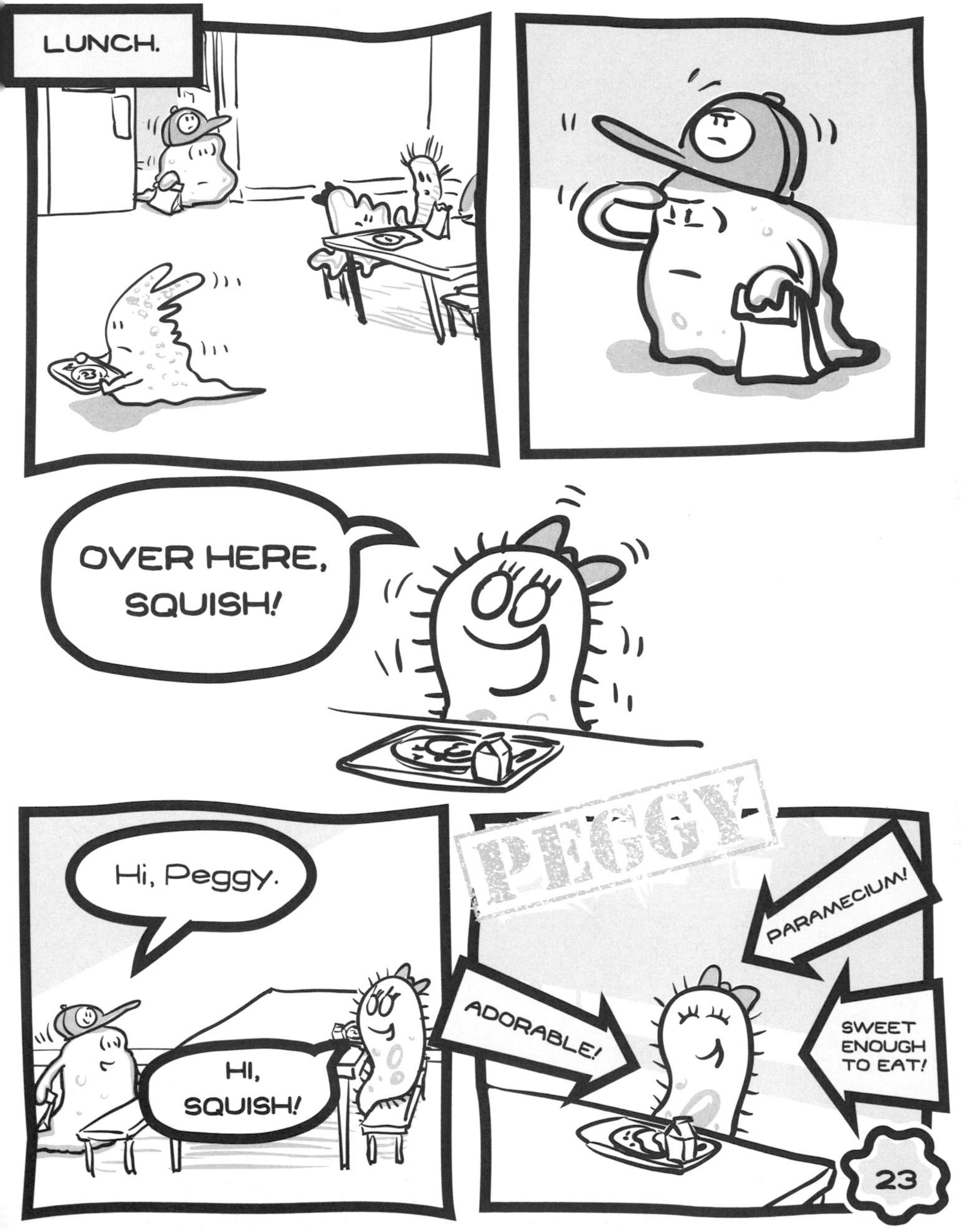
LUNCH.
OVER HERE, SQUISH!
Hi, Peggy.
HI, SQUISH!
PEGGY
PARAMECIUM!
ADORABLE!
SWEET ENOUGH TO EAT!

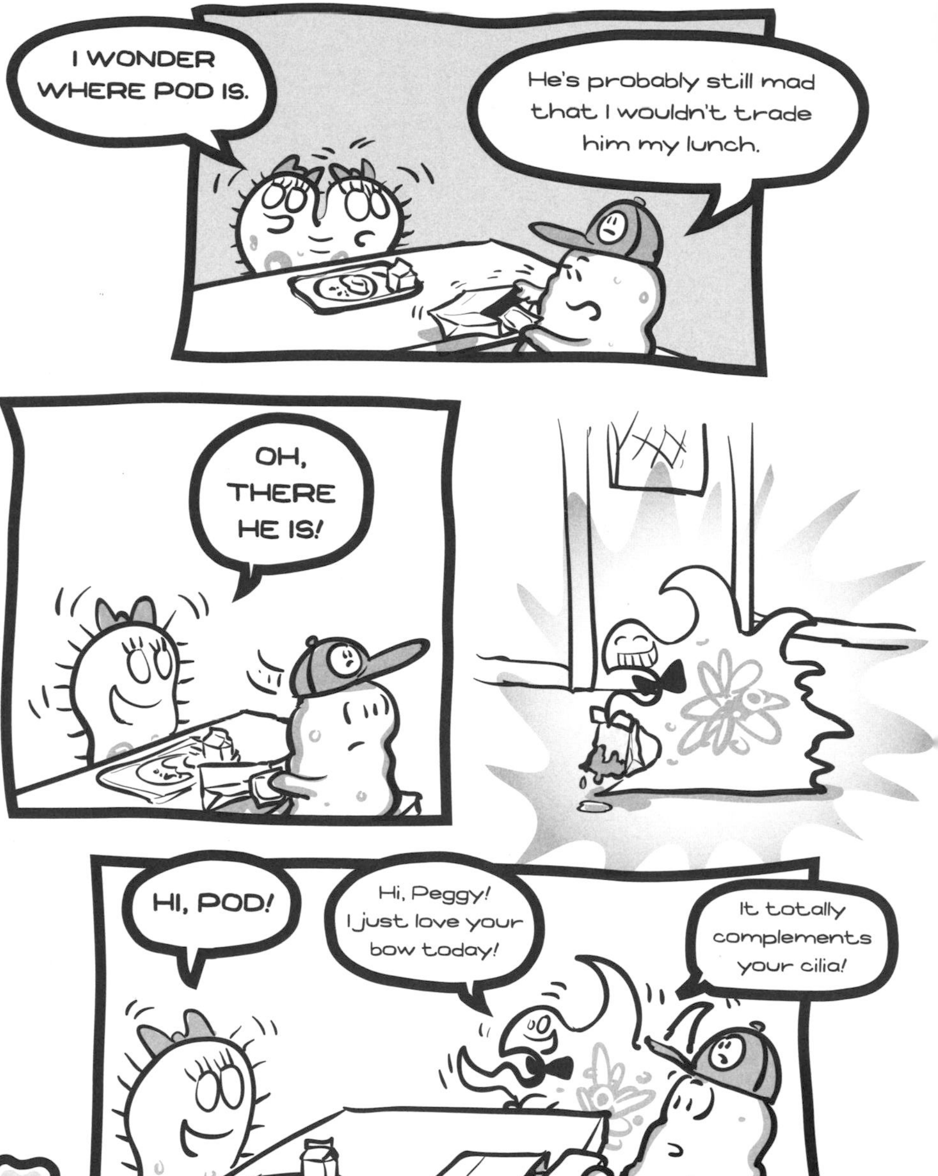
I WONDER WHERE POD IS.
He's probably still mad that I wouldn't trade him my lunch.
OH, THERE HE IS!
HI, POD!
Hi, Peggy! I just love your bow today!
It totally complements your cilia!

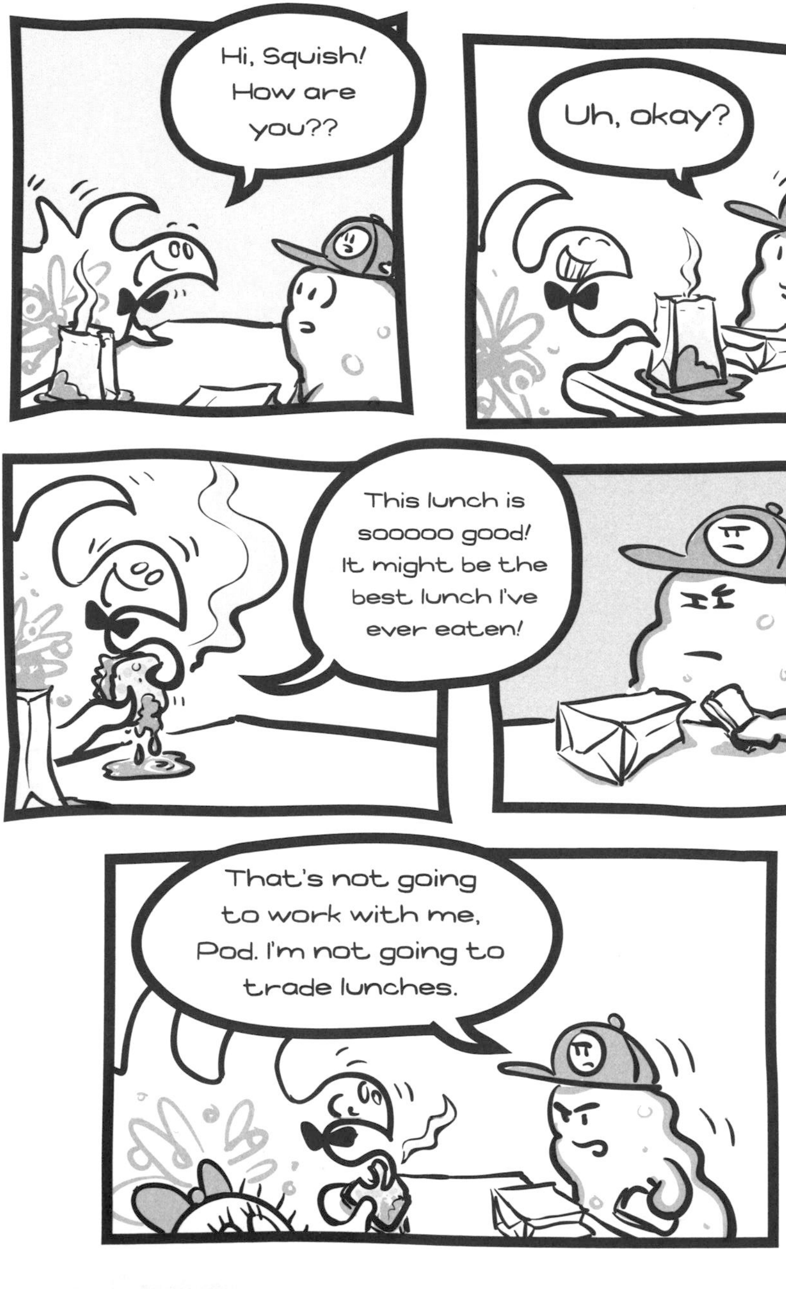
Hi, Squish! How are you??
Uh, okay?
This lunch is sooooo good! It might be the best lunch I've ever eaten!
That's not going to work with me, Pod. I'm not going to trade lunches.

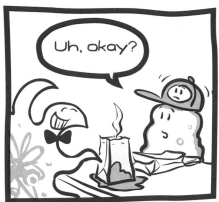

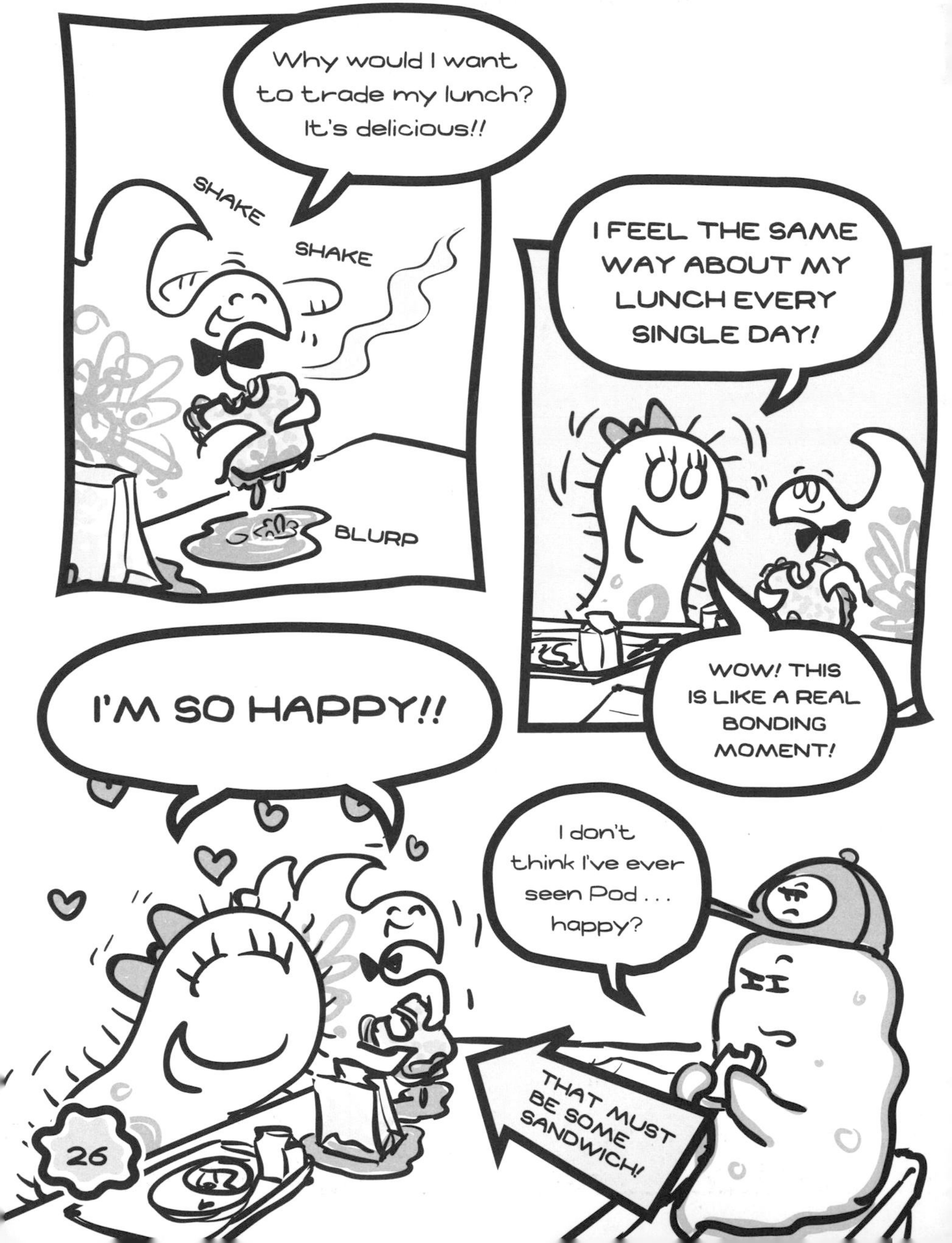
Why would I want to trade my lunch? It's delicious!!
SHAKE
SHAKE
BLURP
I FEEL THE SAME WAY ABOUT MY LUNCH EVERY SINGLE DAY!
WOW! THIS IS LIKE A REAL BONDING MOMENT!
I'M SO HAPPY!!
I don't think I've ever seen Pod . . . happy?
THAT MUST BE SOME SANDWICH!

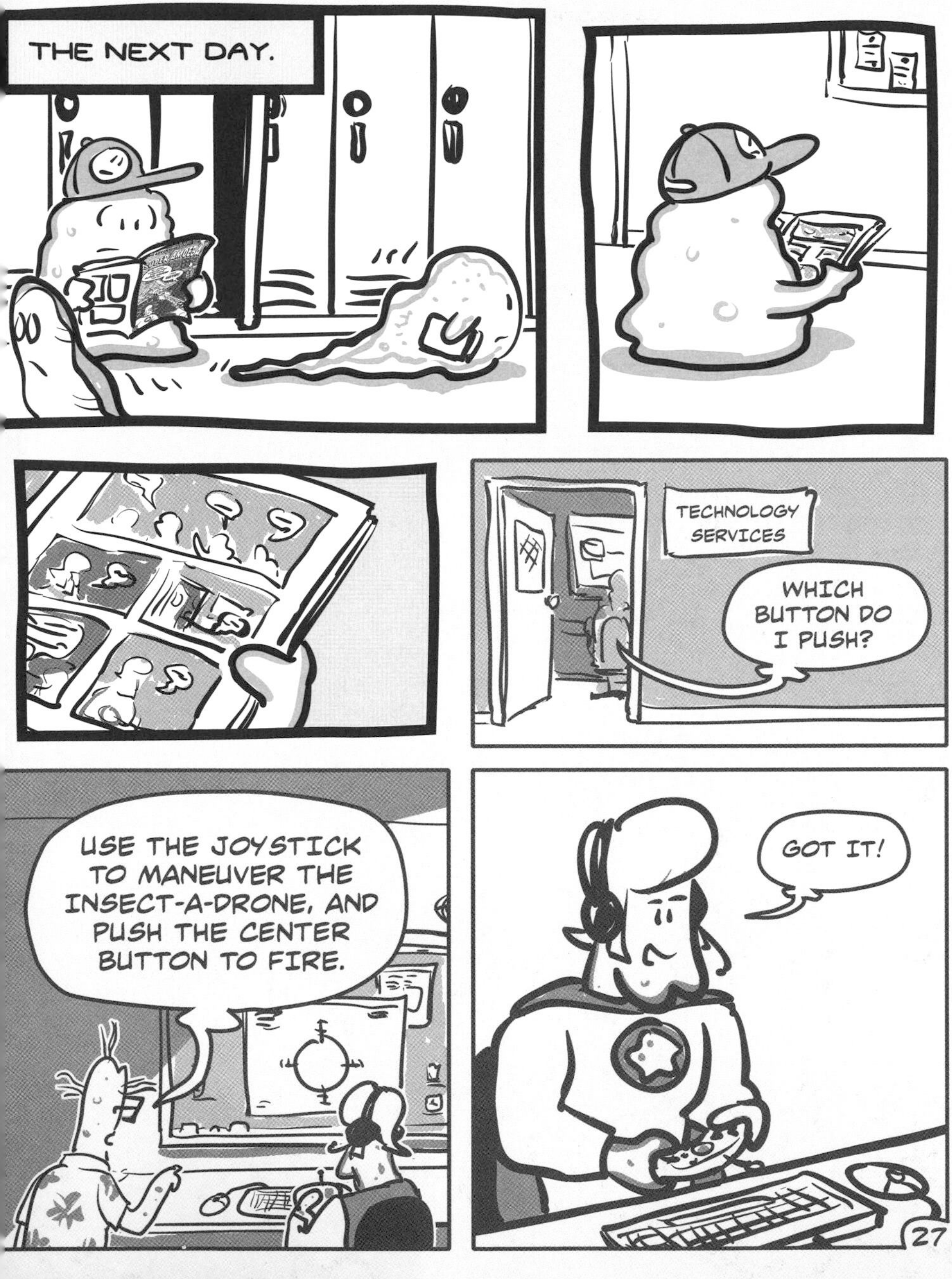
THE NEXT DAY.
SUPER AMOEBA
TECHNOLOGY SERVICES
WHICH BUTTON DO I PUSH?
USE THE JOYSTICK TO MANEUVER THE INSECT-A-DRONE, AND PUSH THE CENTER BUTTON TO FIRE.
GOT IT!

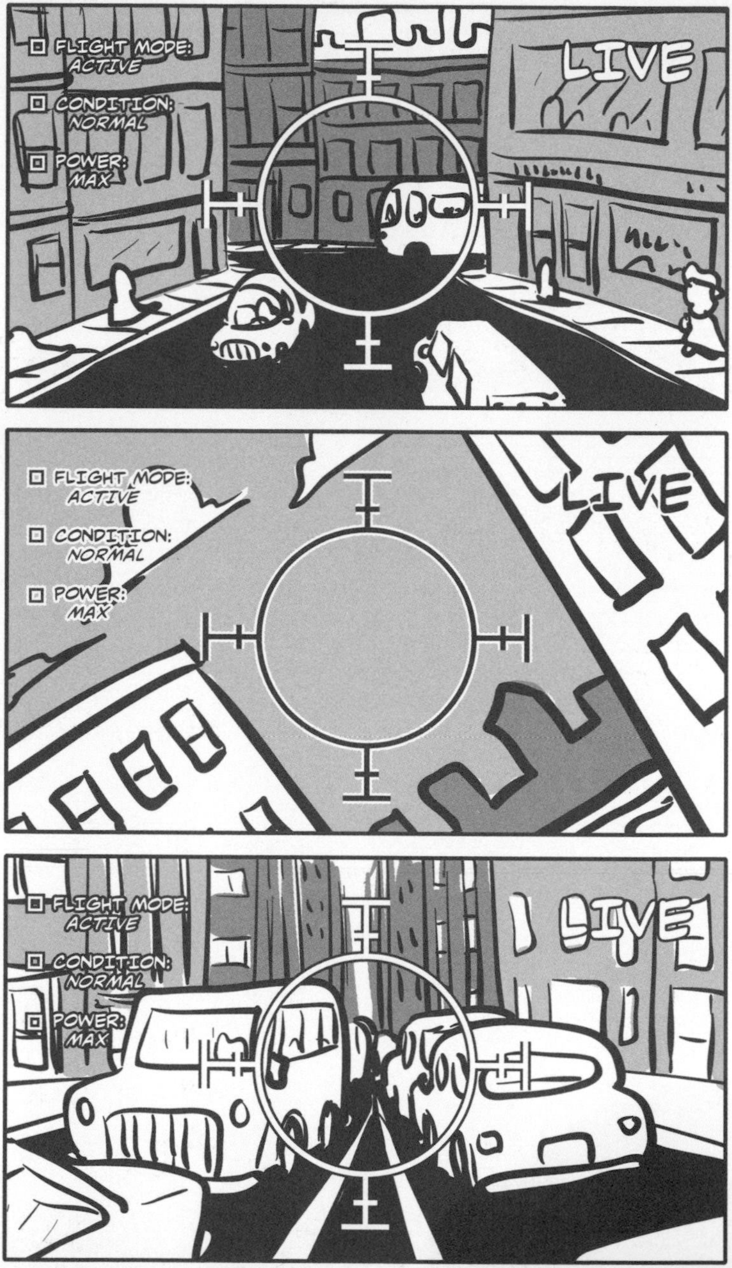
FLIGHT MODE: ACTIVE
CONDITION: NORMAL
POWER: MAX
LIVE
FLIGHT MODE: ACTIVE
CONDITION: NORMAL
POWER: MAX
LIVE
FLIGHT MODE: ACTIVE
CONDITION: NORMAL
POWER: MAX
LIVE

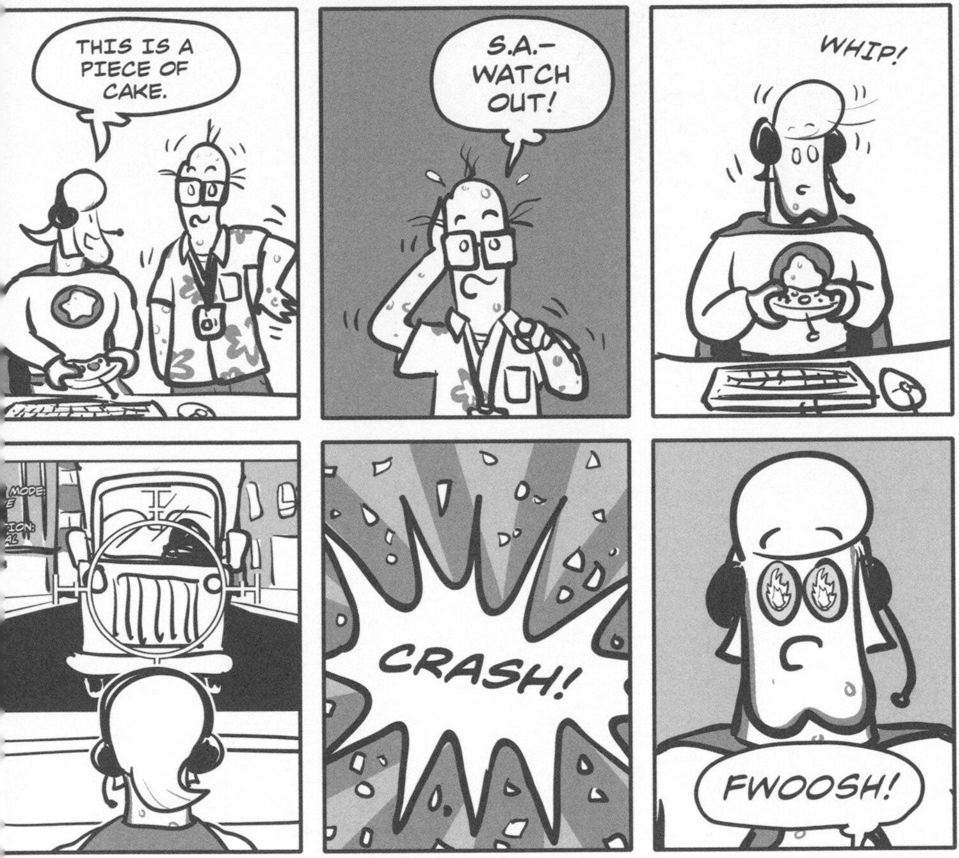
THIS IS A PIECE OF CAKE.
S.A.- WATCH OUT!
WHIP!
CRASH!
FWOOSH!

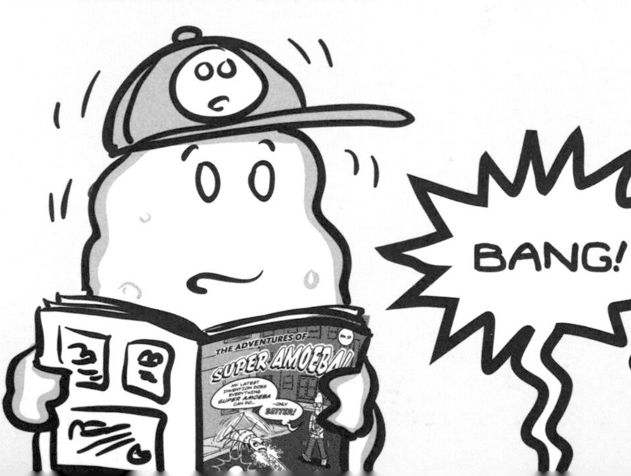
THE ADVENTURES OF
BANG!

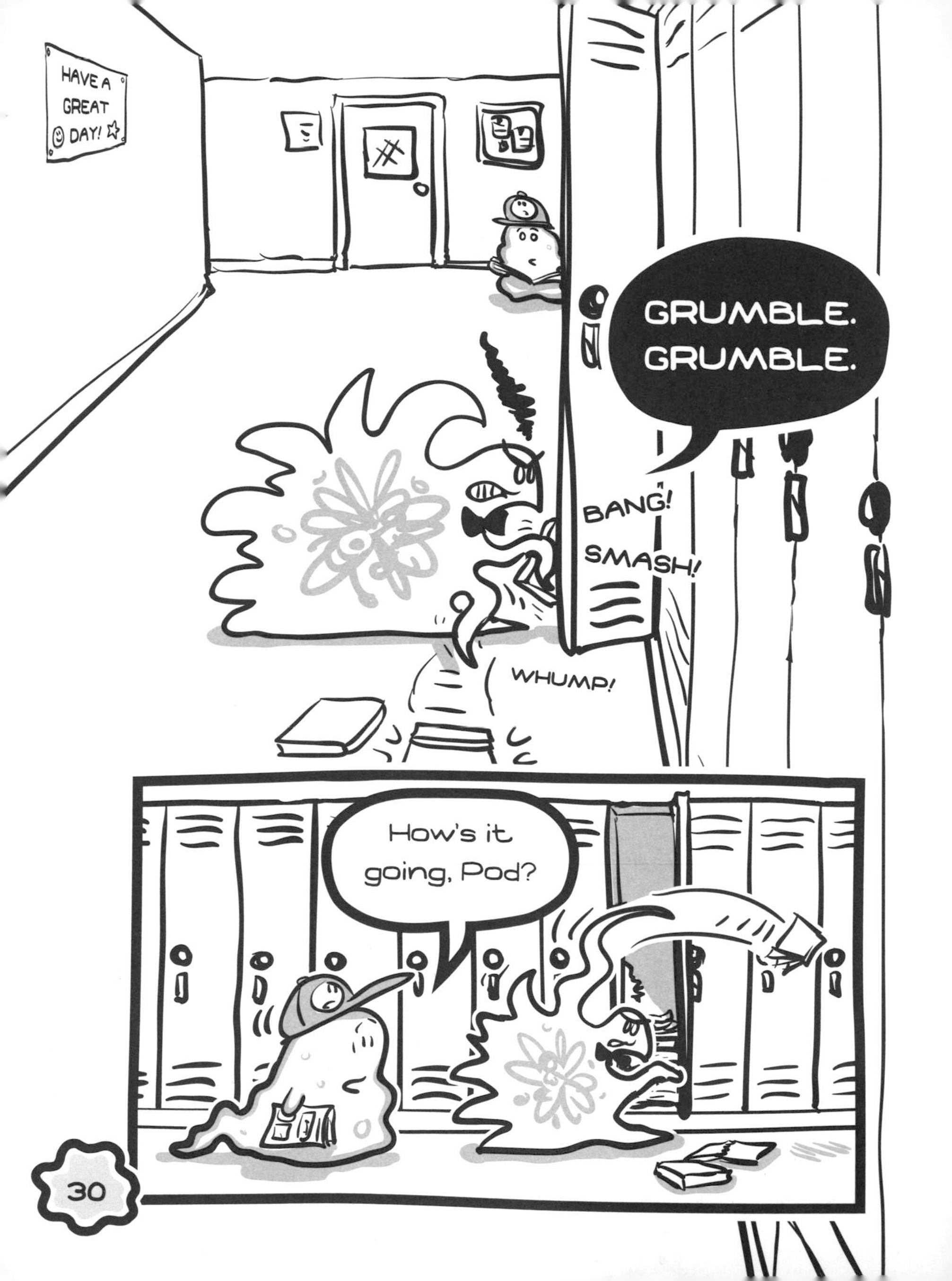

HAVE A GREAT DAY!
GRUMBLE. GRUMBLE.
BANG!
SMASH!
WHUMP!
How's it going, Pod?

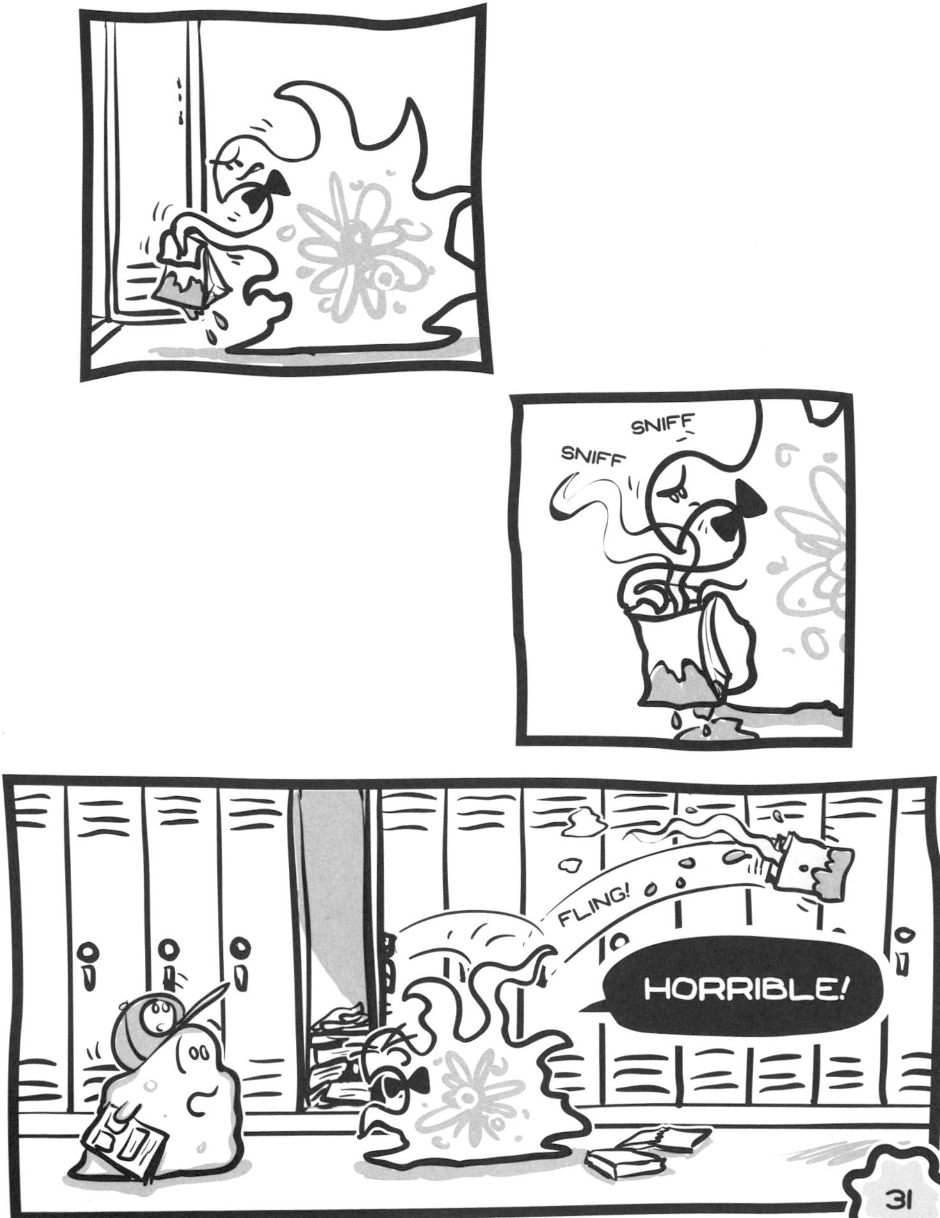
SNIFF
SNIFF
FLING!
HORRIBLE!

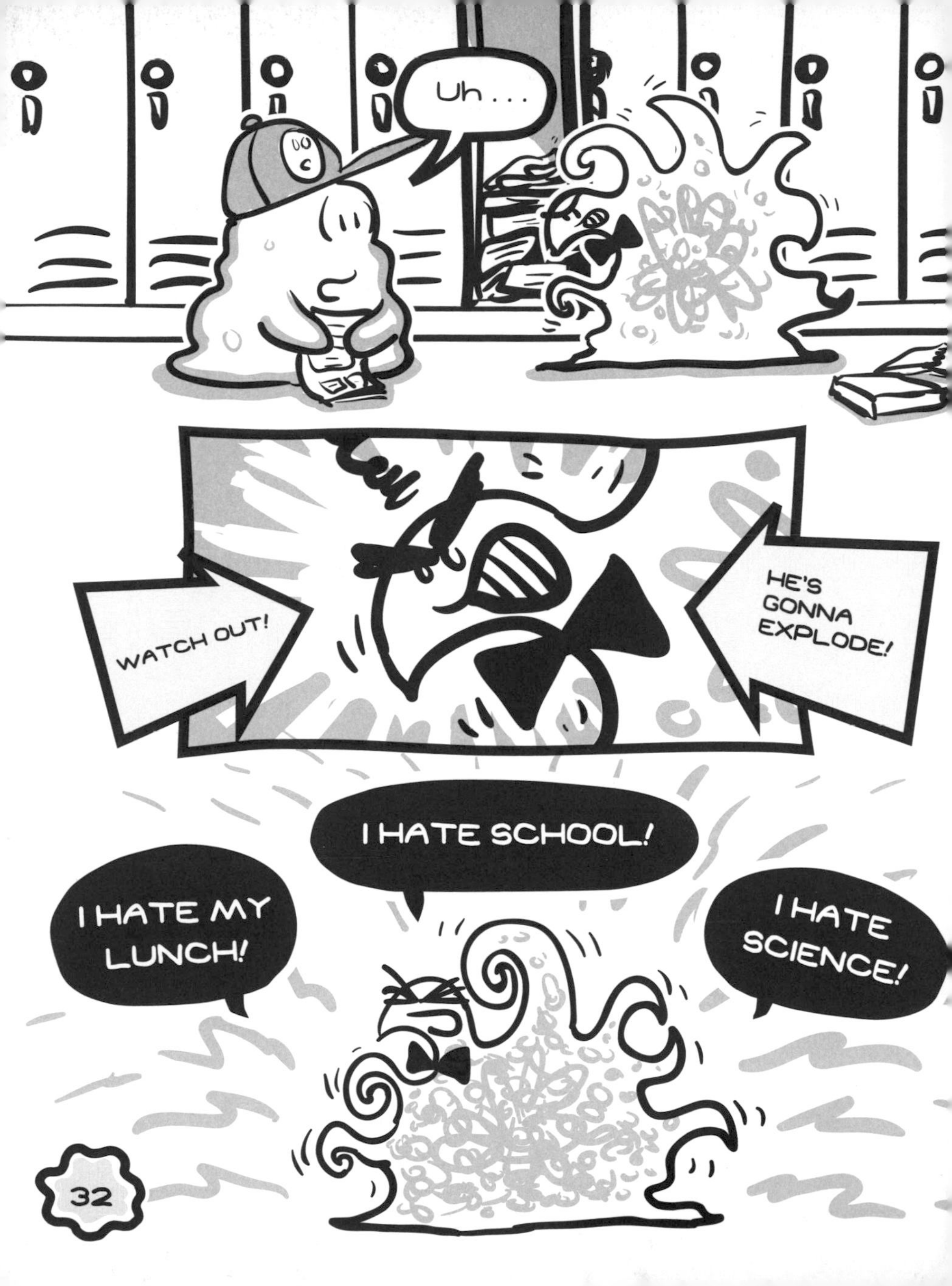
Uh . . .
WATCH OUT!
HE'S GONNA EXPLODE!
I HATE SCHOOL!
I HATE MY LUNCH!
I HATE SCIENCE!

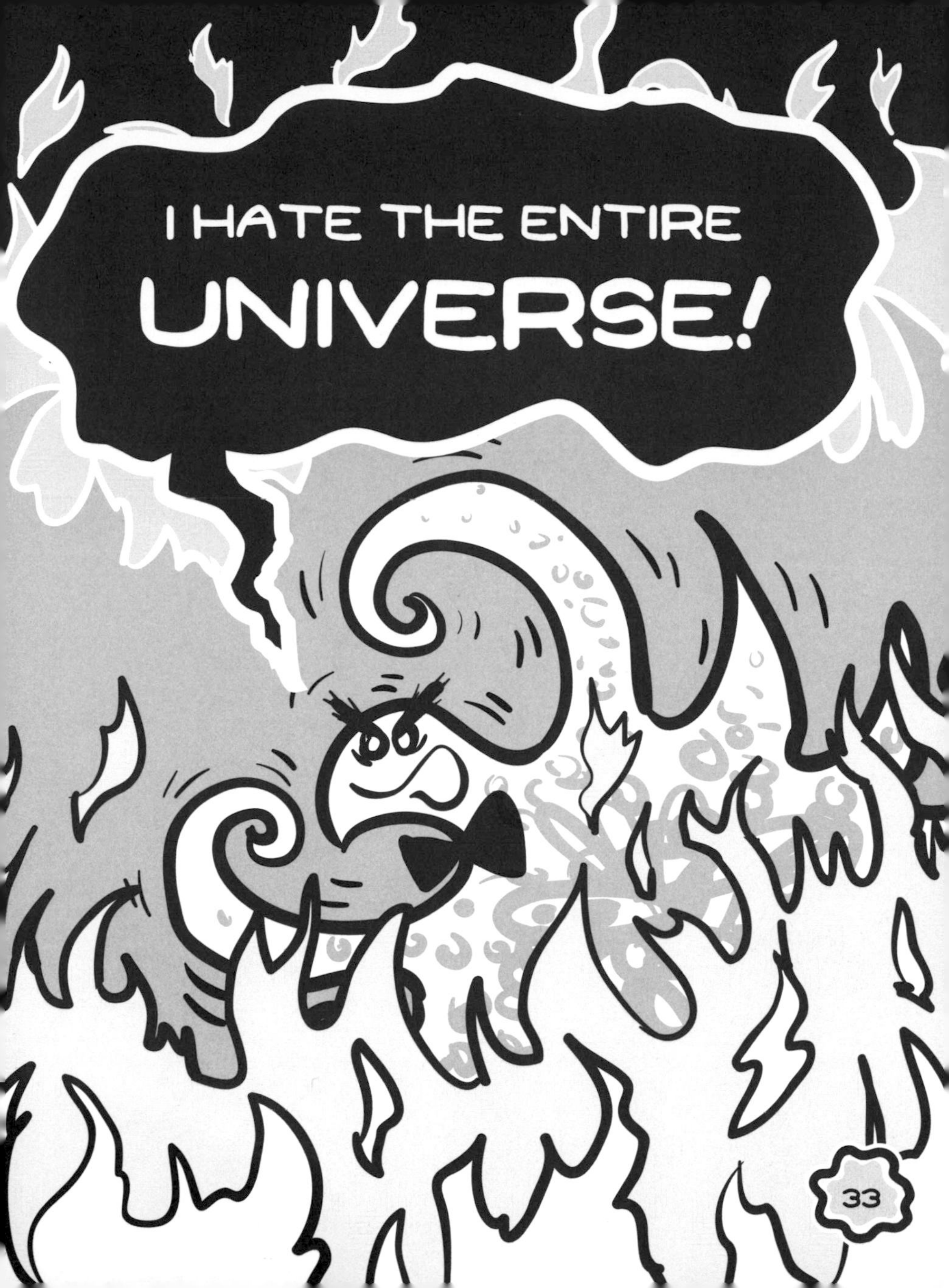
I HATE THE ENTIRE
UNIVERSE!

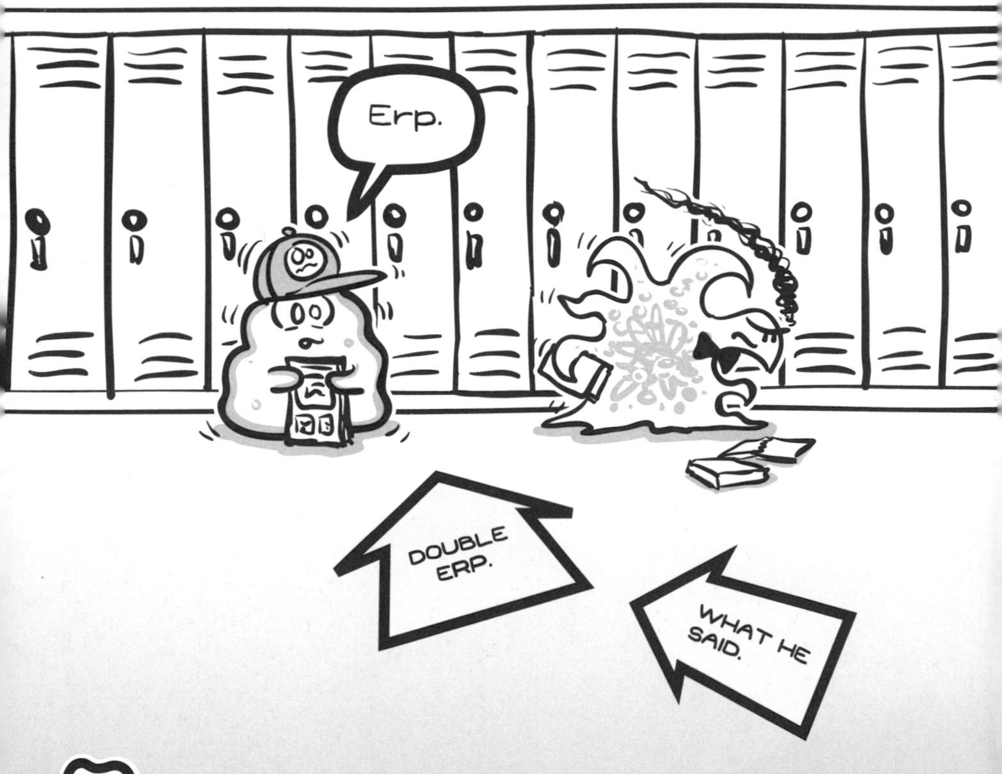
Erp.
DOUBLE ERP.
WHAT HE SAID.

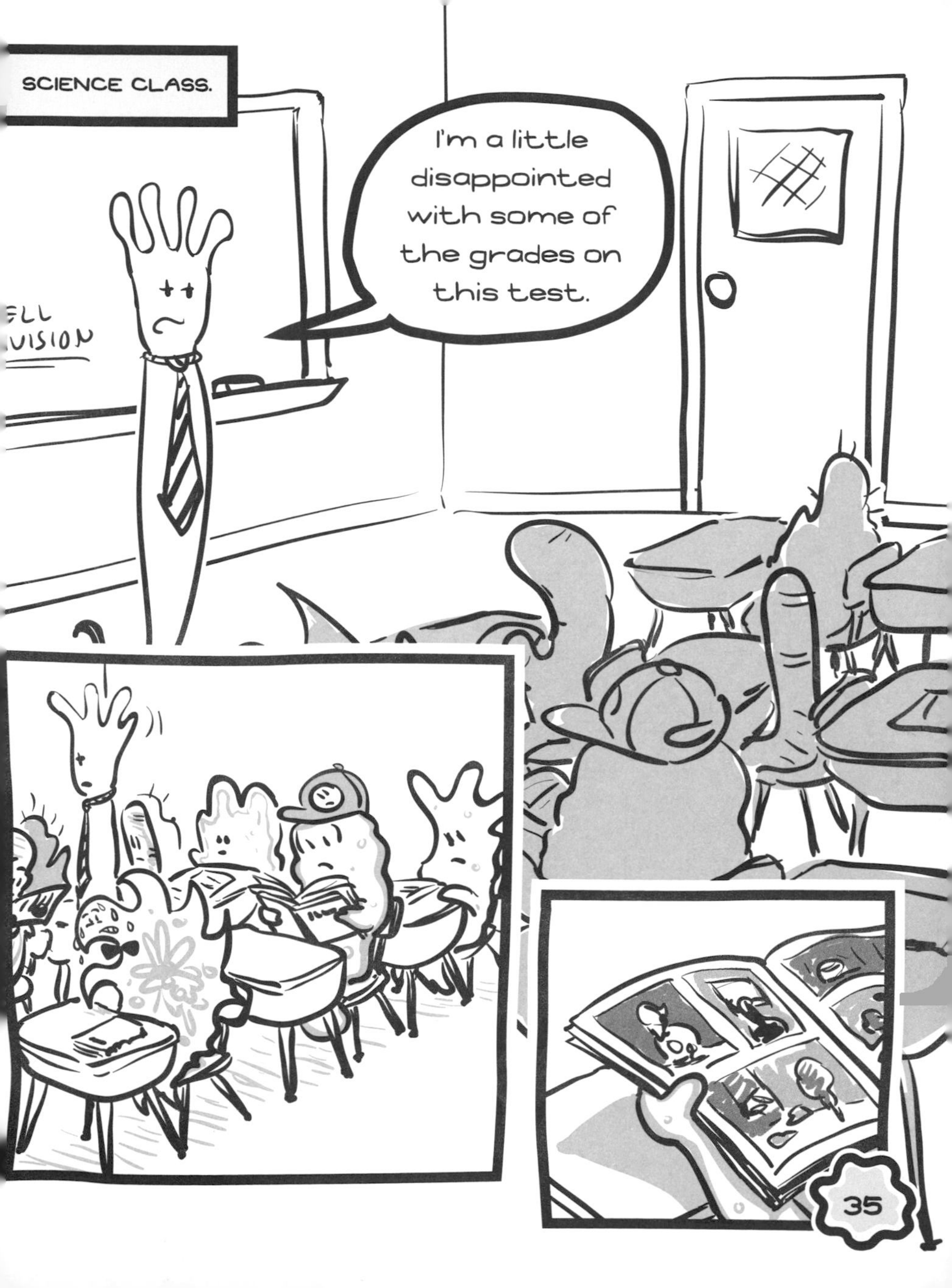
SCIENCE CLASS.
I'm a little disappointed with some of the grades on this test.
ELL
VISION
35

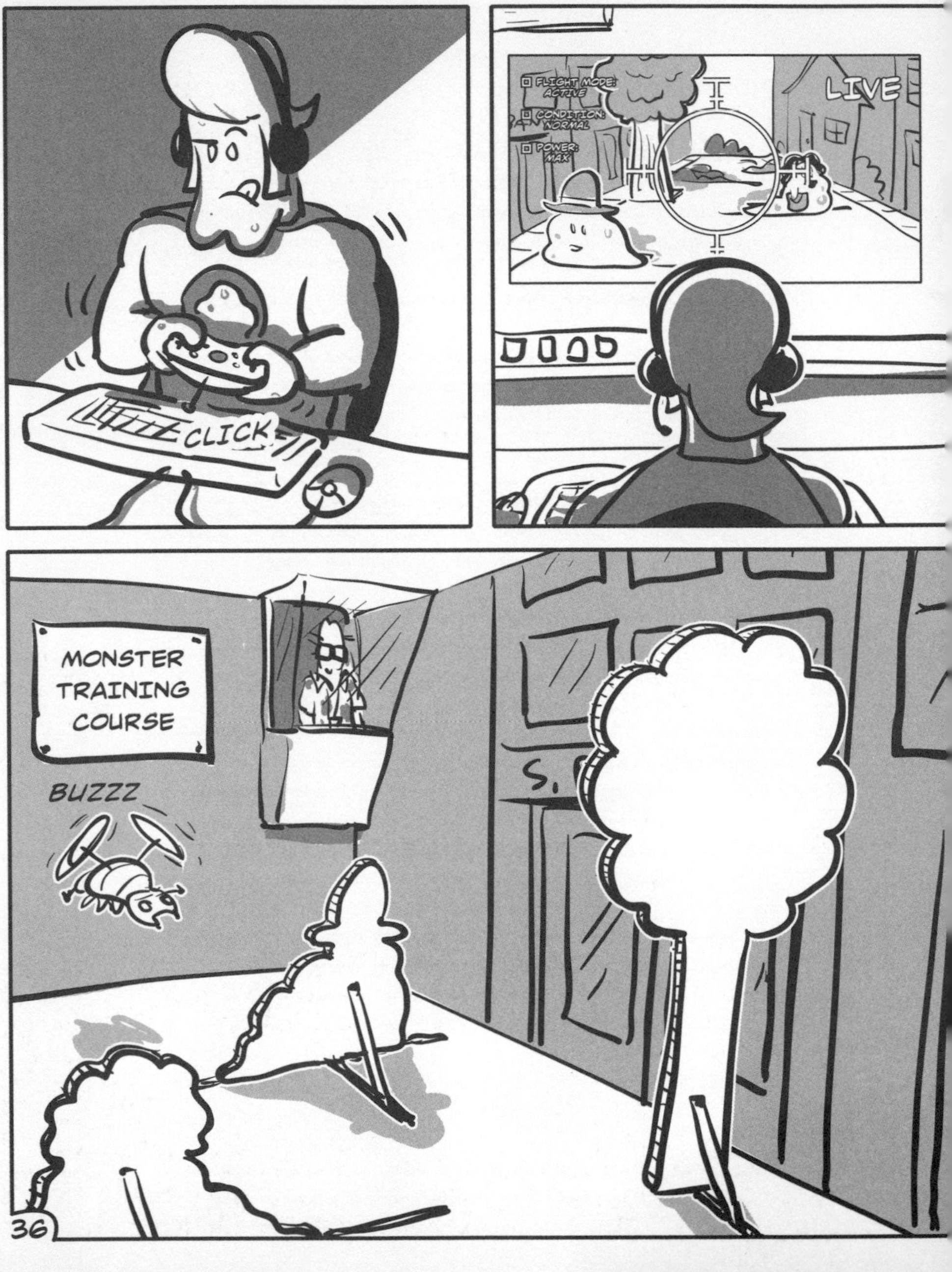
CLICK
FLIGHT MODE: ACTIVE
CONDITION: NORMAL
POWER: MAX
LIVE
MONSTER TRAINING COURSE
BUZZZ

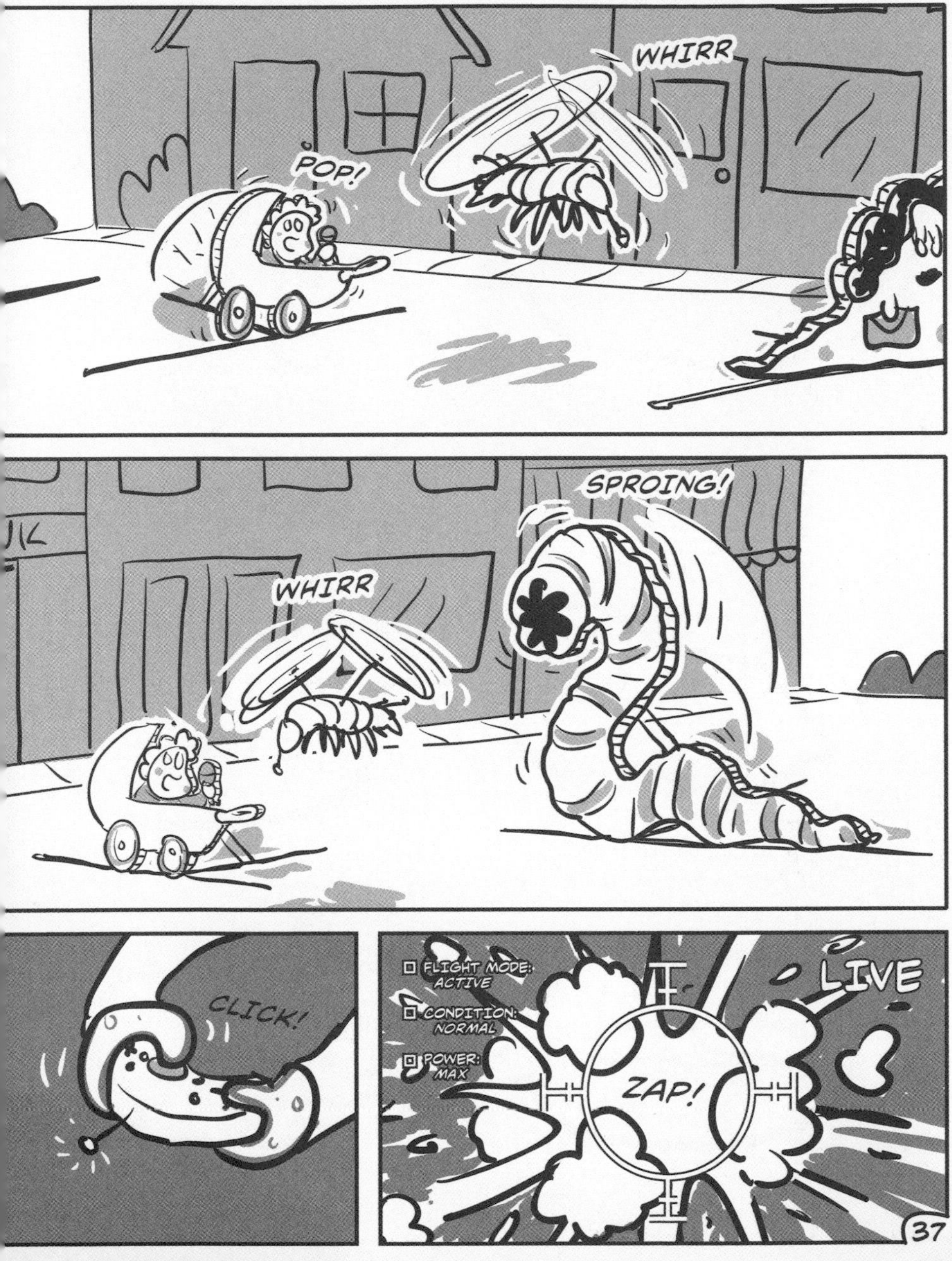
WHIRR
POP!
SPROING!
WHIRR
CLICK!
FLIGHT MODE: ACTIVE
CONDITION: NORMAL
POWER: MAX
LIVE
ZAP!

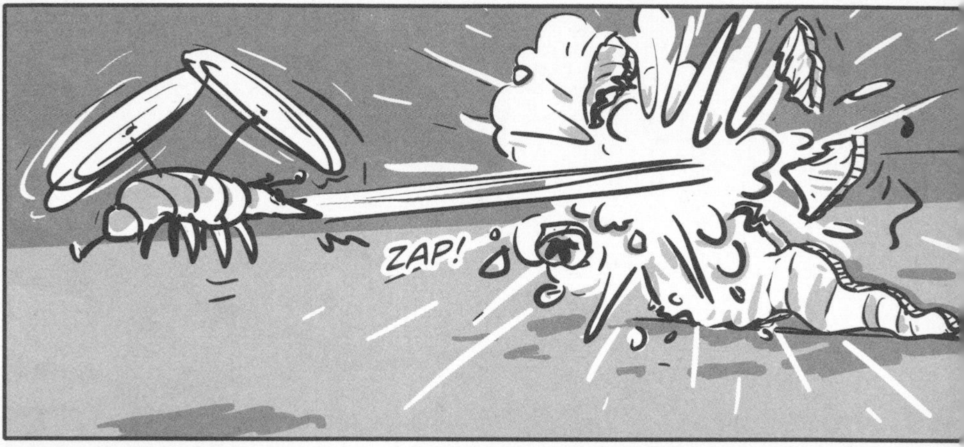
ZAP!

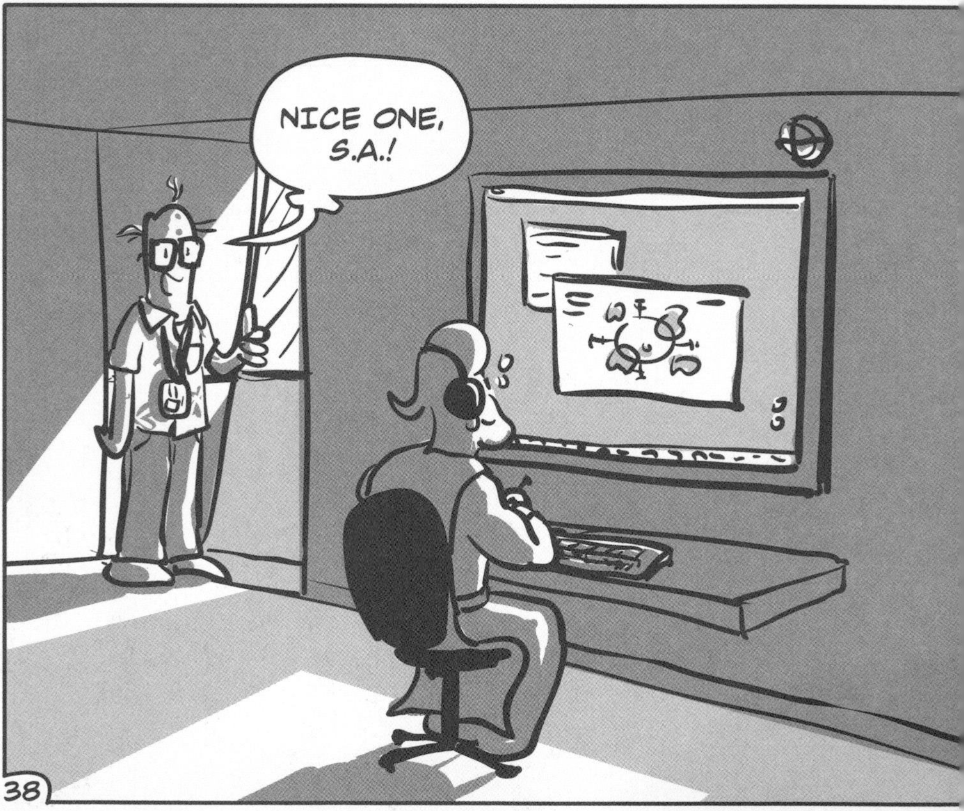
NICE ONE, S.A.!

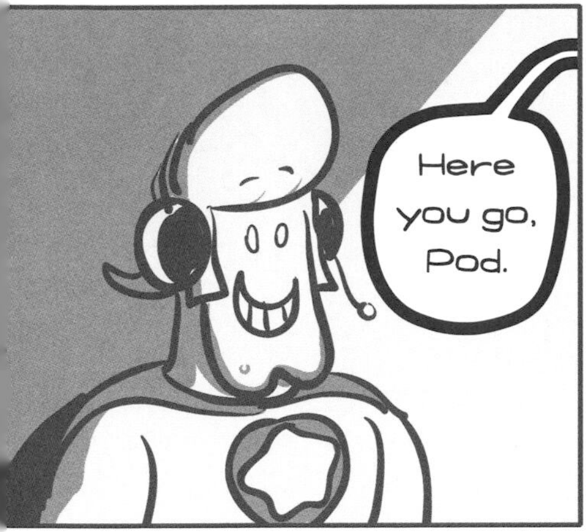
Here you go, Pod.

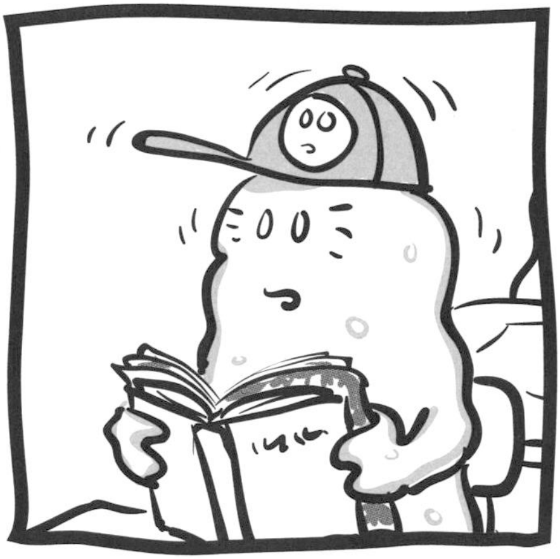

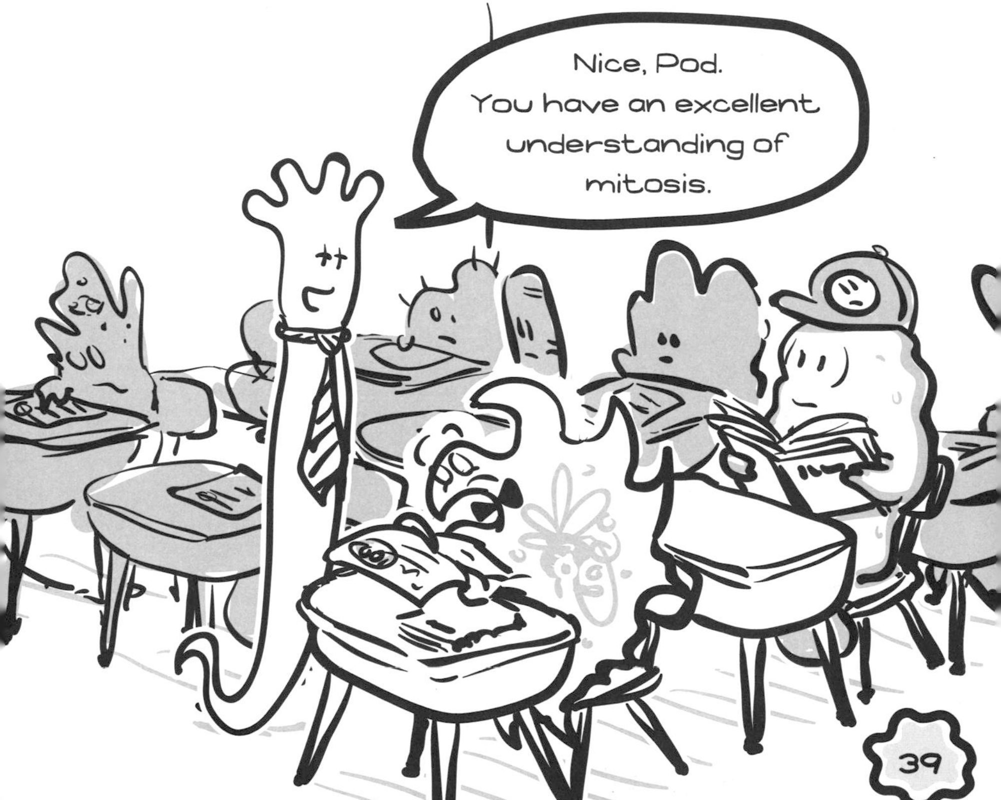
Nice, Pod.
You have an excellent understanding of mitosis.

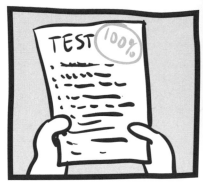

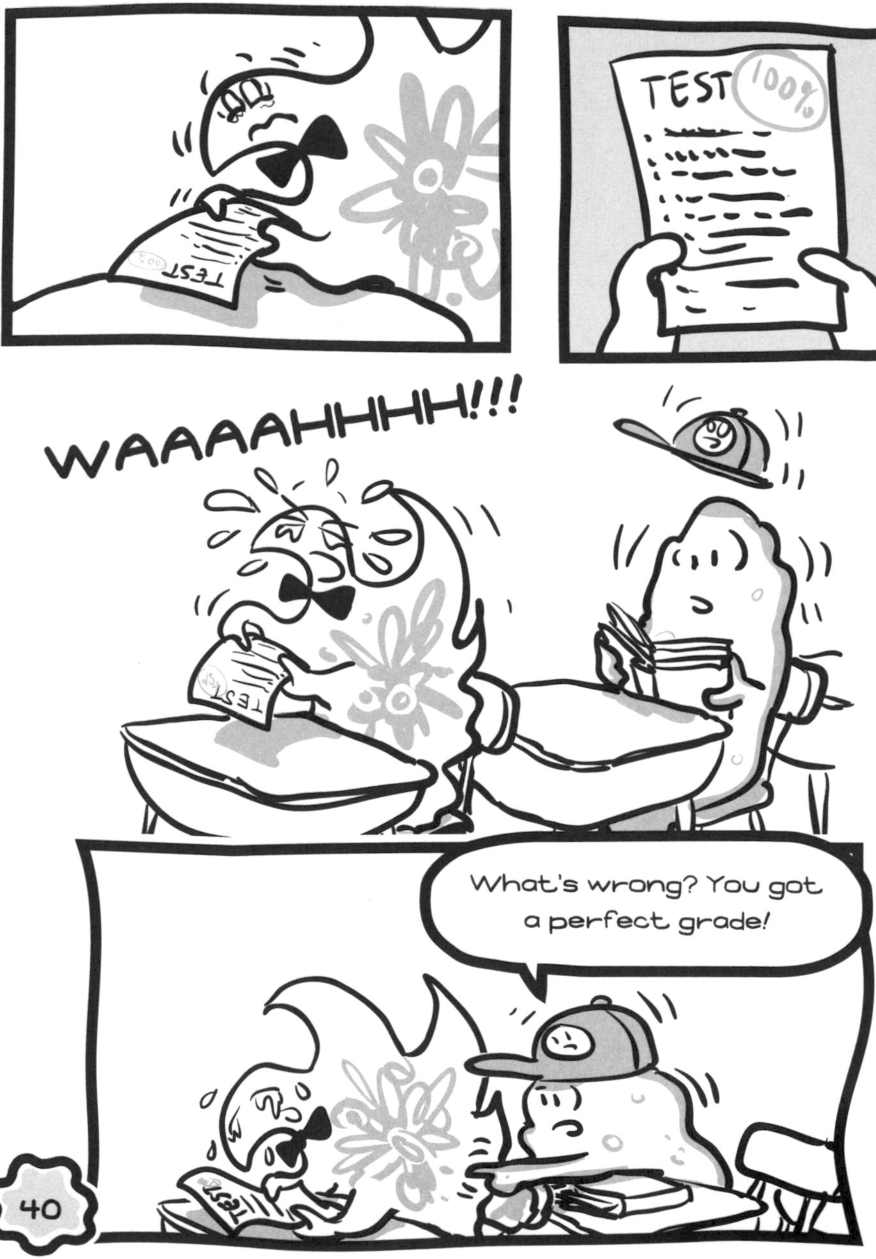
TEST 100%
TEST 100%
WAAAAHHHH!!!
TEST
What's wrong? You got a perfect grade!
TEST

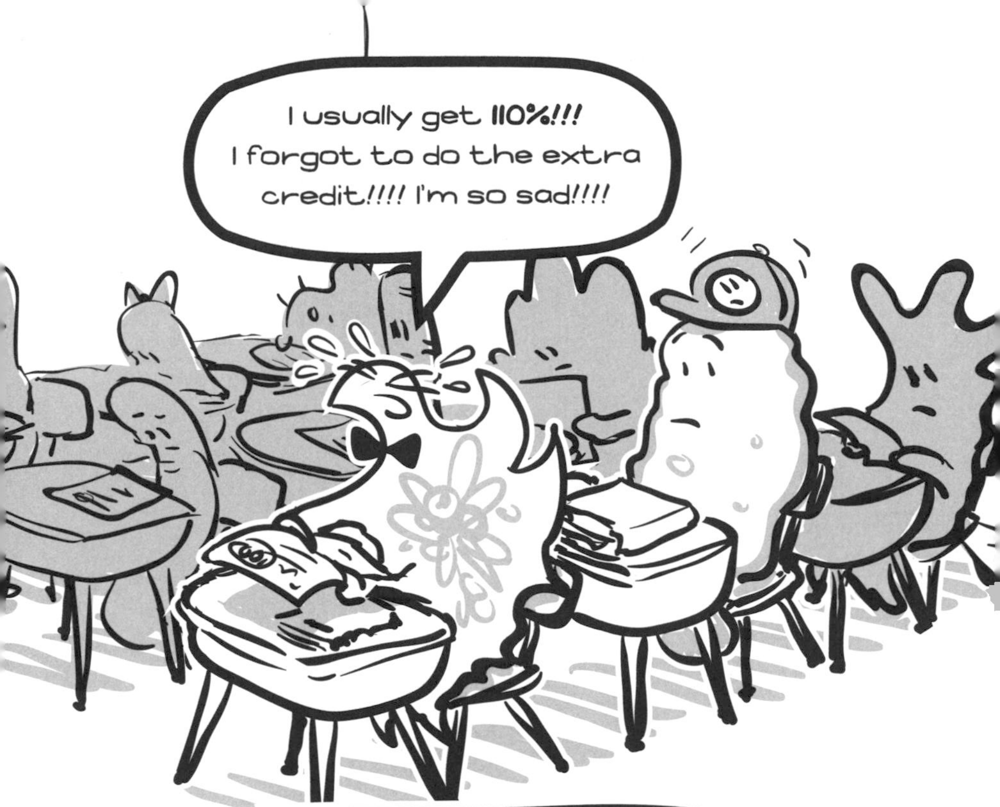
I usually get 110%!!!
I forgot to do the extra credit!!!! I'm so sad!!!!

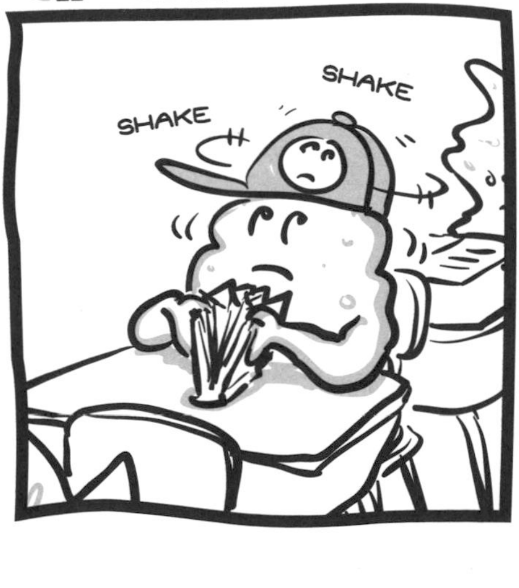
SHAKE
SHAKE

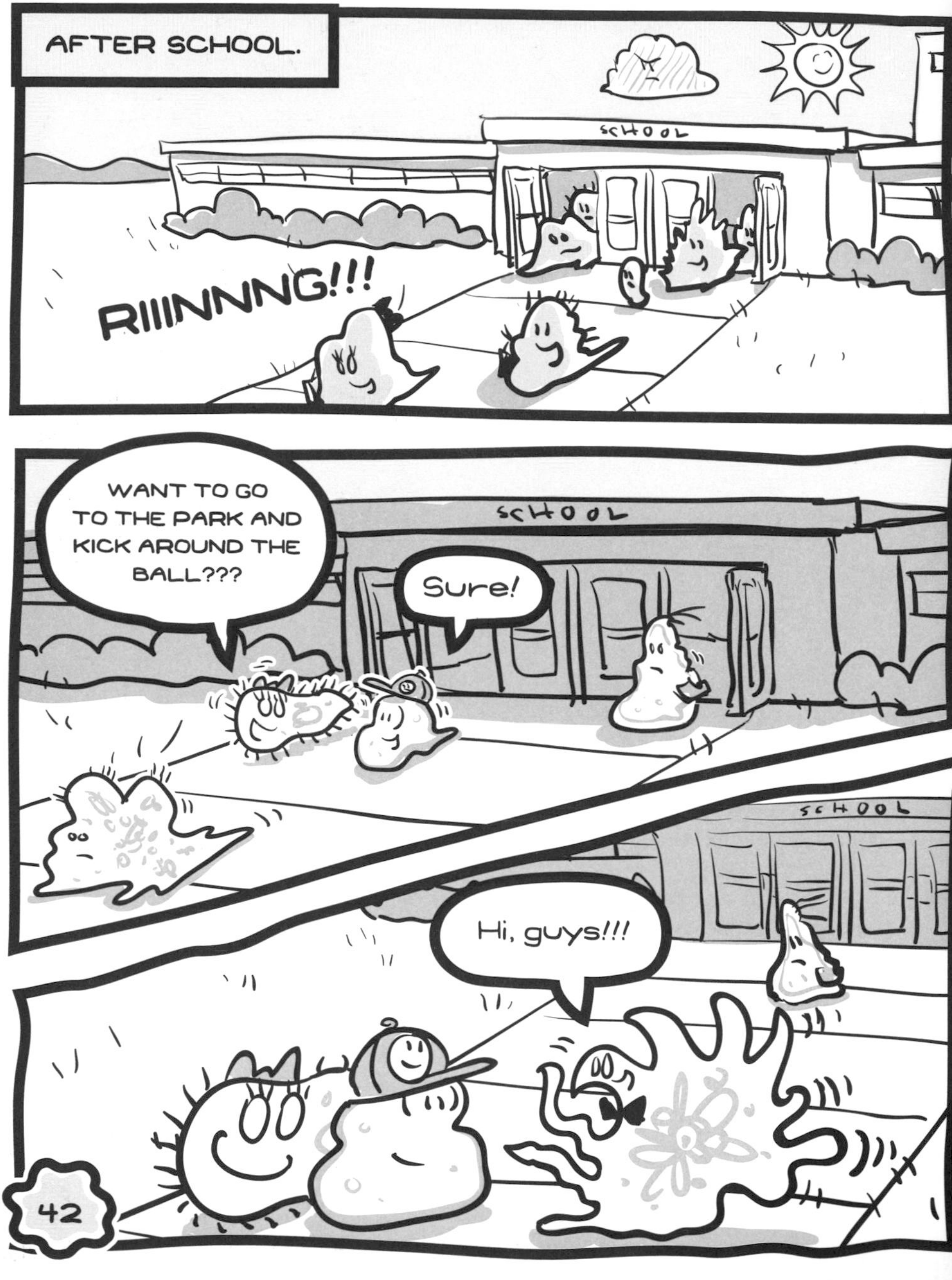

AFTER SCHOOL.
SCHOOL
RIIINNNG!!!
SCHOOL
WANT TO GO TO THE PARK AND KICK AROUND THE BALL???
Sure!
SCHOOL
Hi, guys!!!

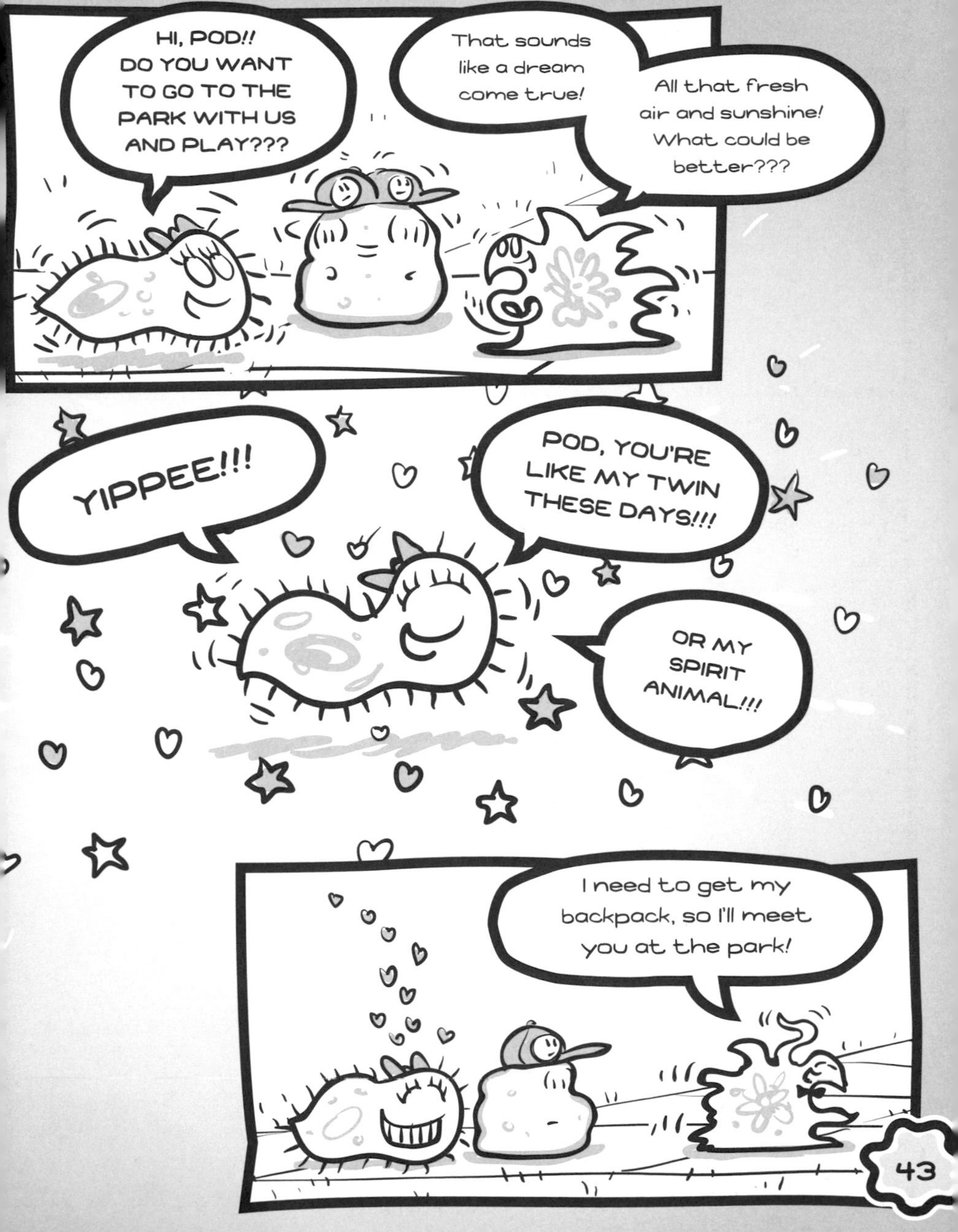
HI, POD!! DO YOU WANT TO GO TO THE PARK WITH US AND PLAY???
That sounds like a dream come true!
All that fresh air and sunshine! What could be better???
YIPPEE!!!
POD, YOU'RE LIKE MY TWIN THESE DAYS!!!
OR MY SPIRIT ANIMAL!!!
I need to get my backpack, so I'll meet you at the park!

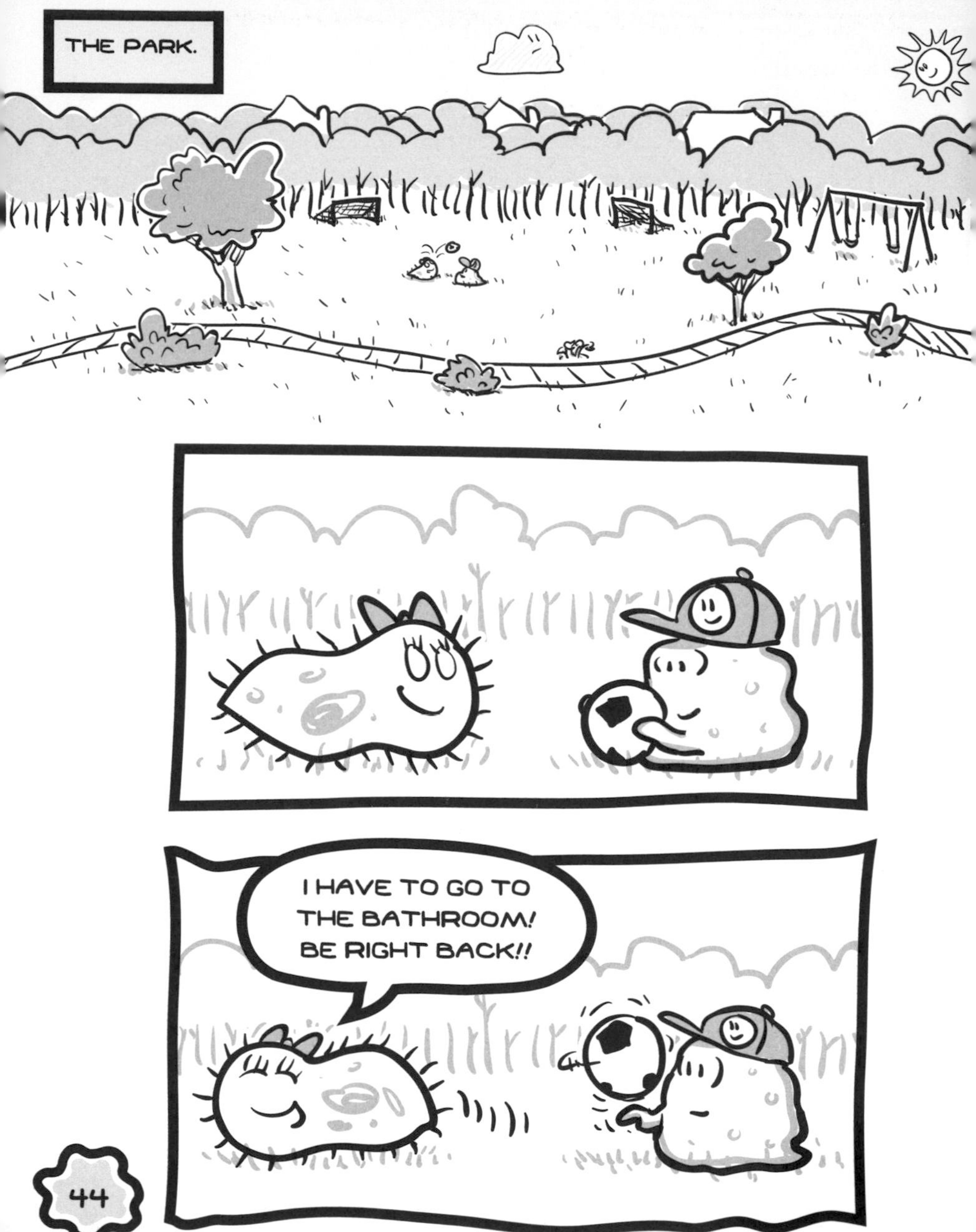
THE PARK.
I HAVE TO GO TO THE BATHROOM! BE RIGHT BACK!!

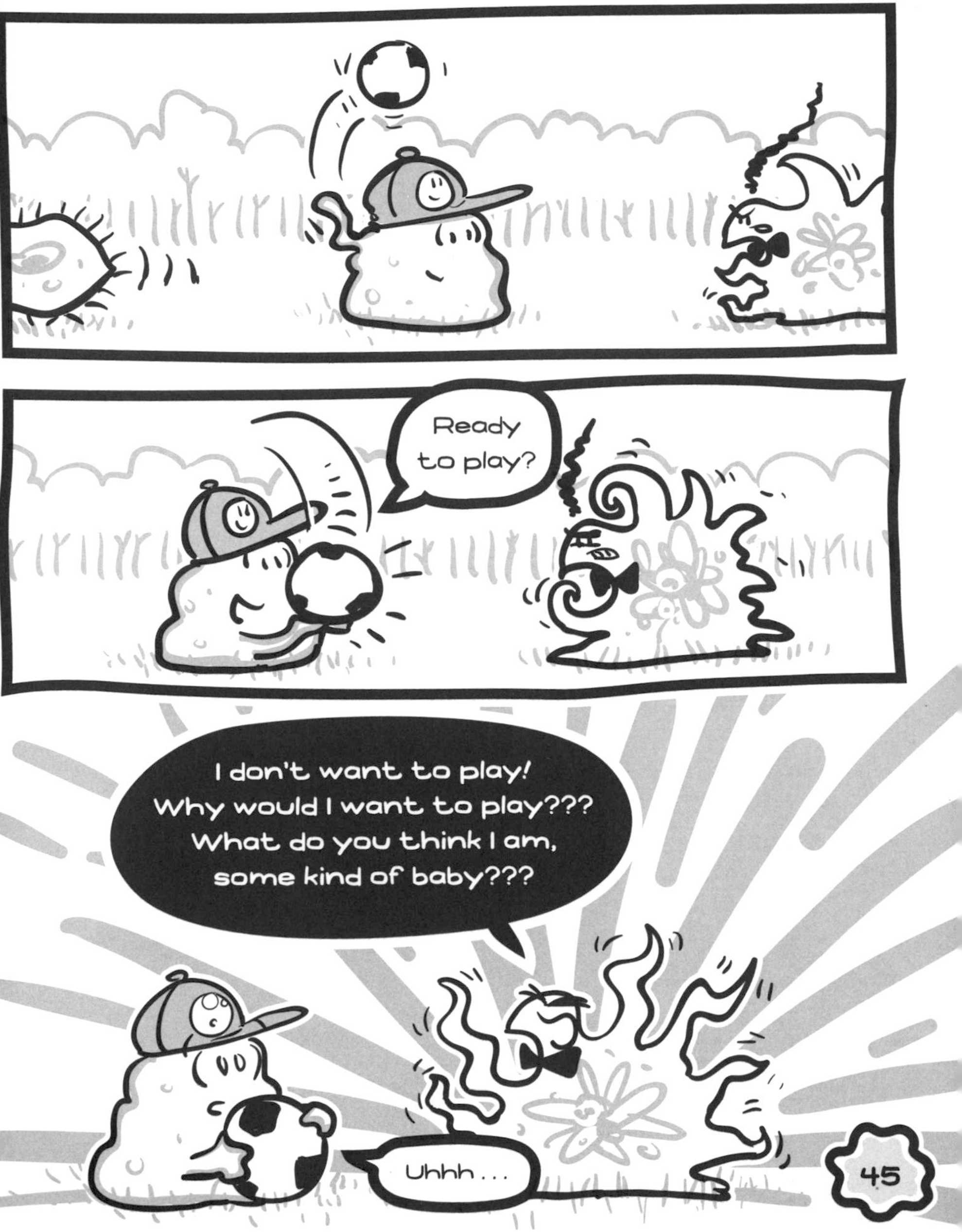
Ready to play?
I don't want to play!
Why would I want to play???
What do you think I am,
some kind of baby???
Uhhh . . .

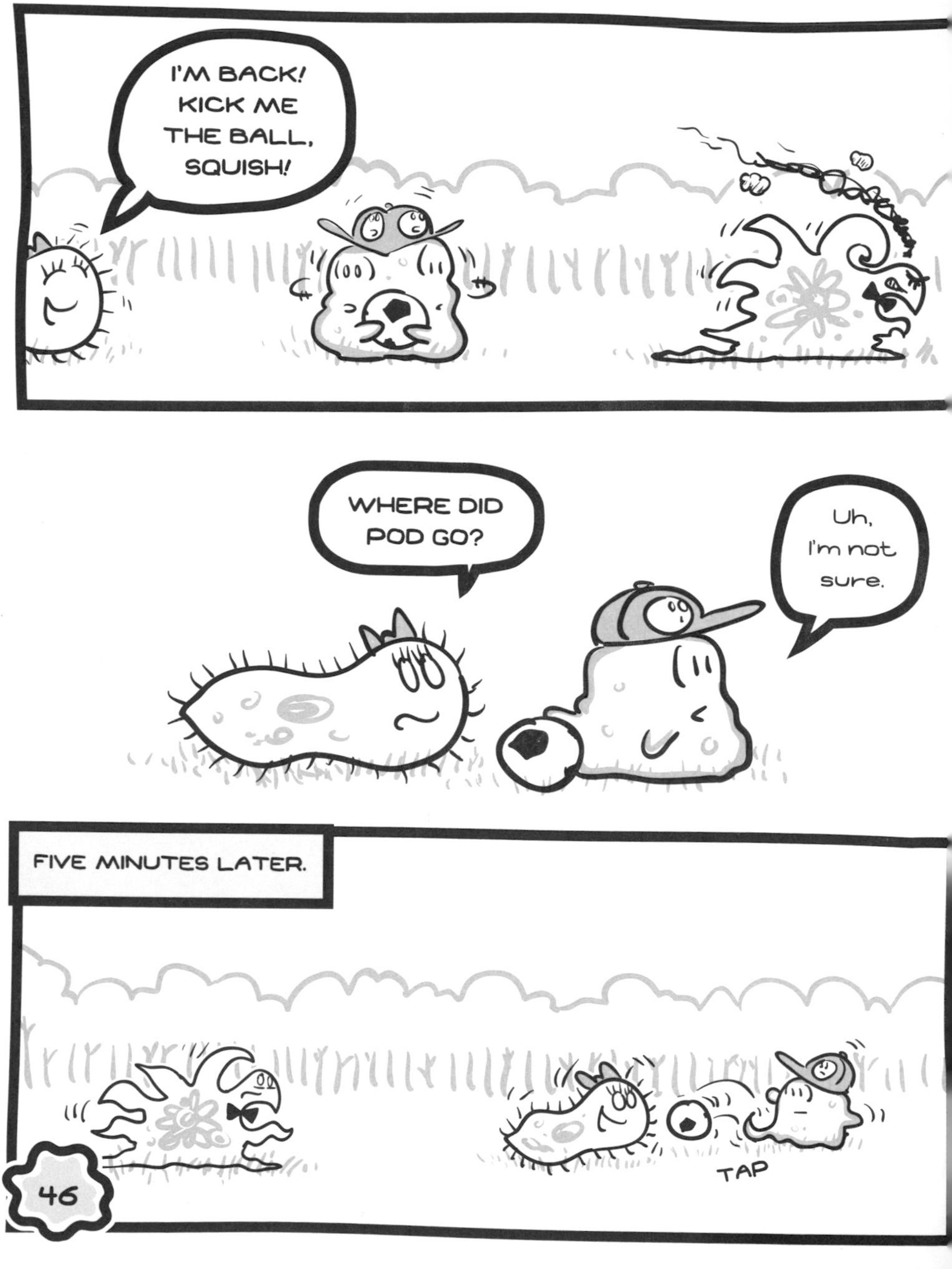
I'M BACK! KICK ME THE BALL, SQUISH!
WHERE DID POD GO?
Uh, I'm not sure.
FIVE MINUTES LATER.
TAP

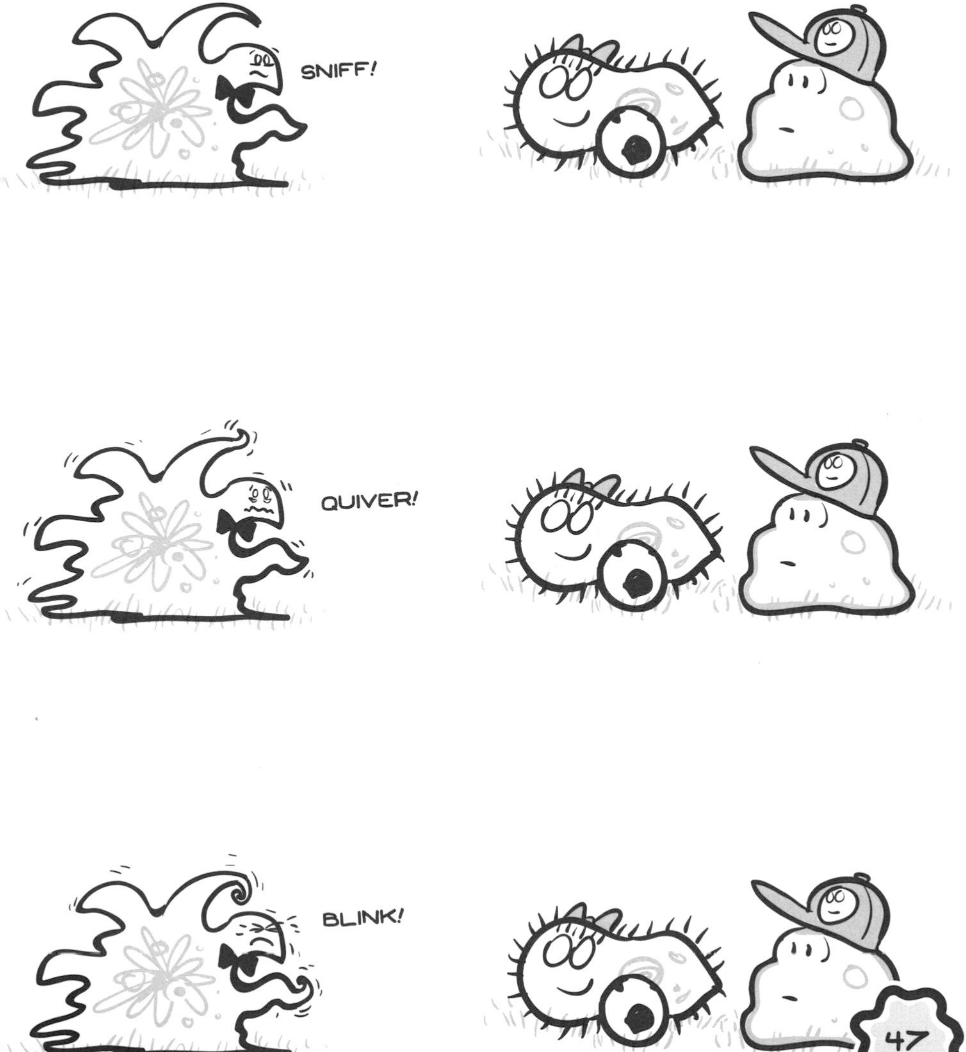
SNIFF!
QUIVER!
BLINK!

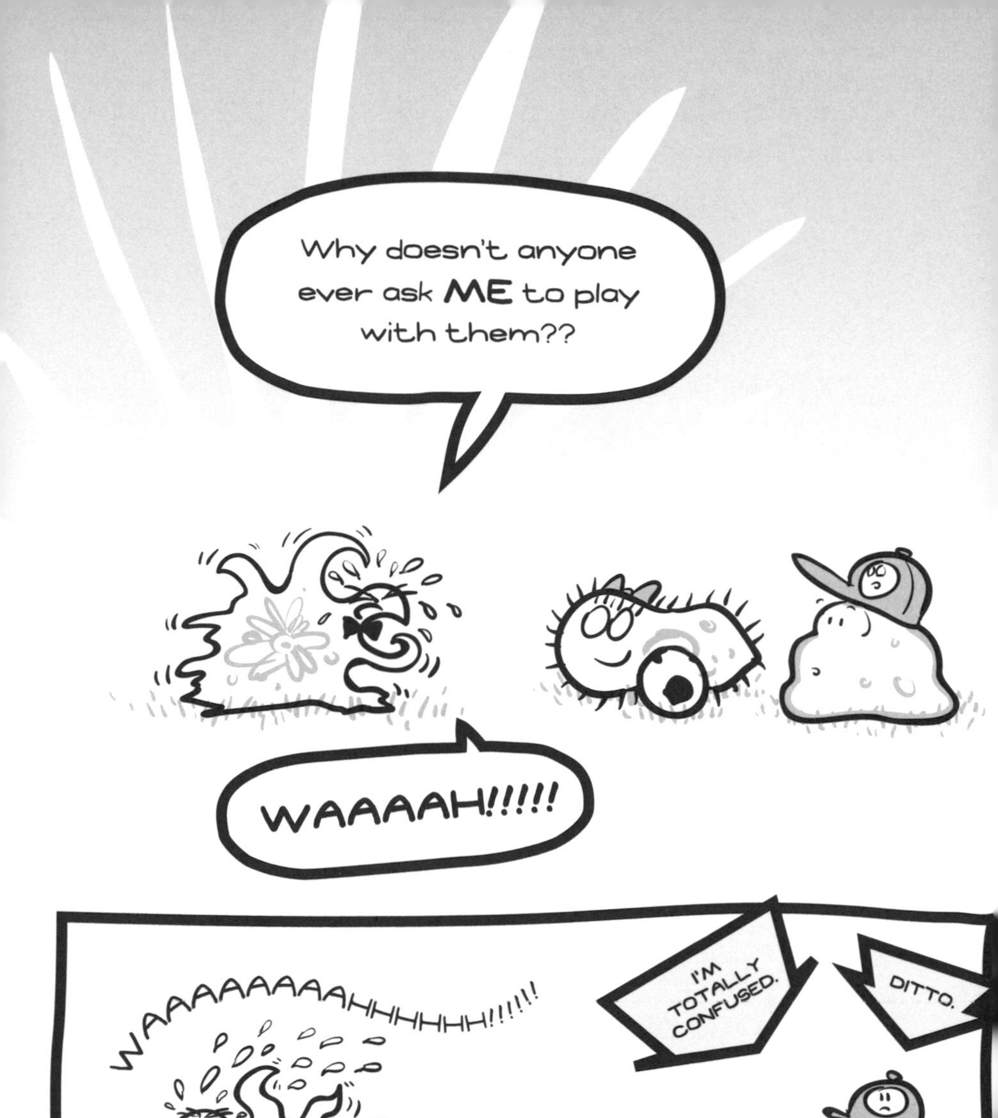
Why doesn't anyone ever ask **ME** to play with them??
WAAAAH!!!!!
WAAAAAAAAHHHHHH!!!!!!
I'M TOTALLY CONFUSED.
DITTO.

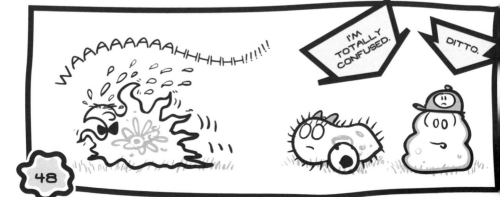

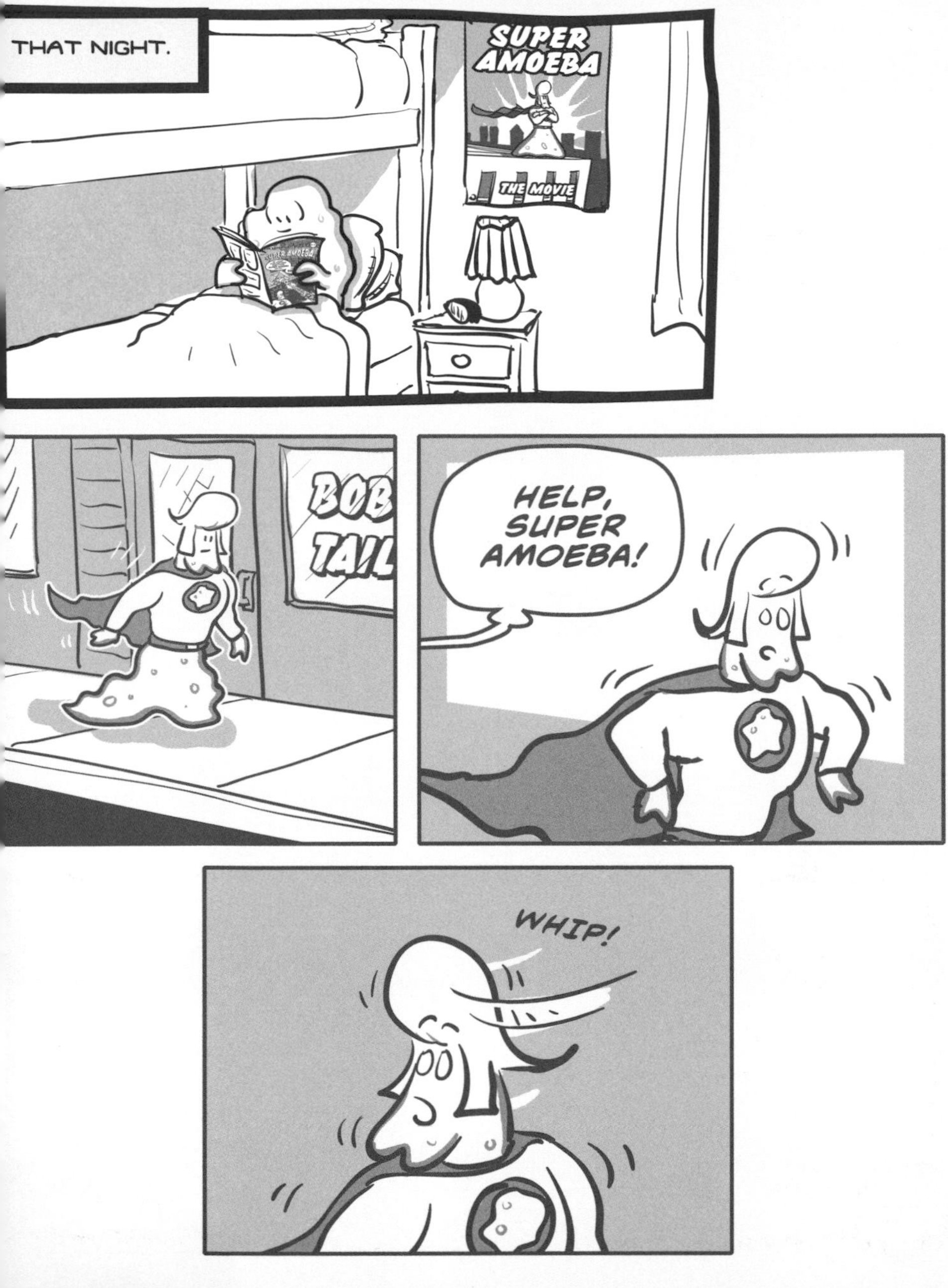
THAT NIGHT.
SUPER AMOEBA
THE MOVIE
SUPER AMOEBA
BOB
HELP, SUPER AMOEBA!
WHIP!

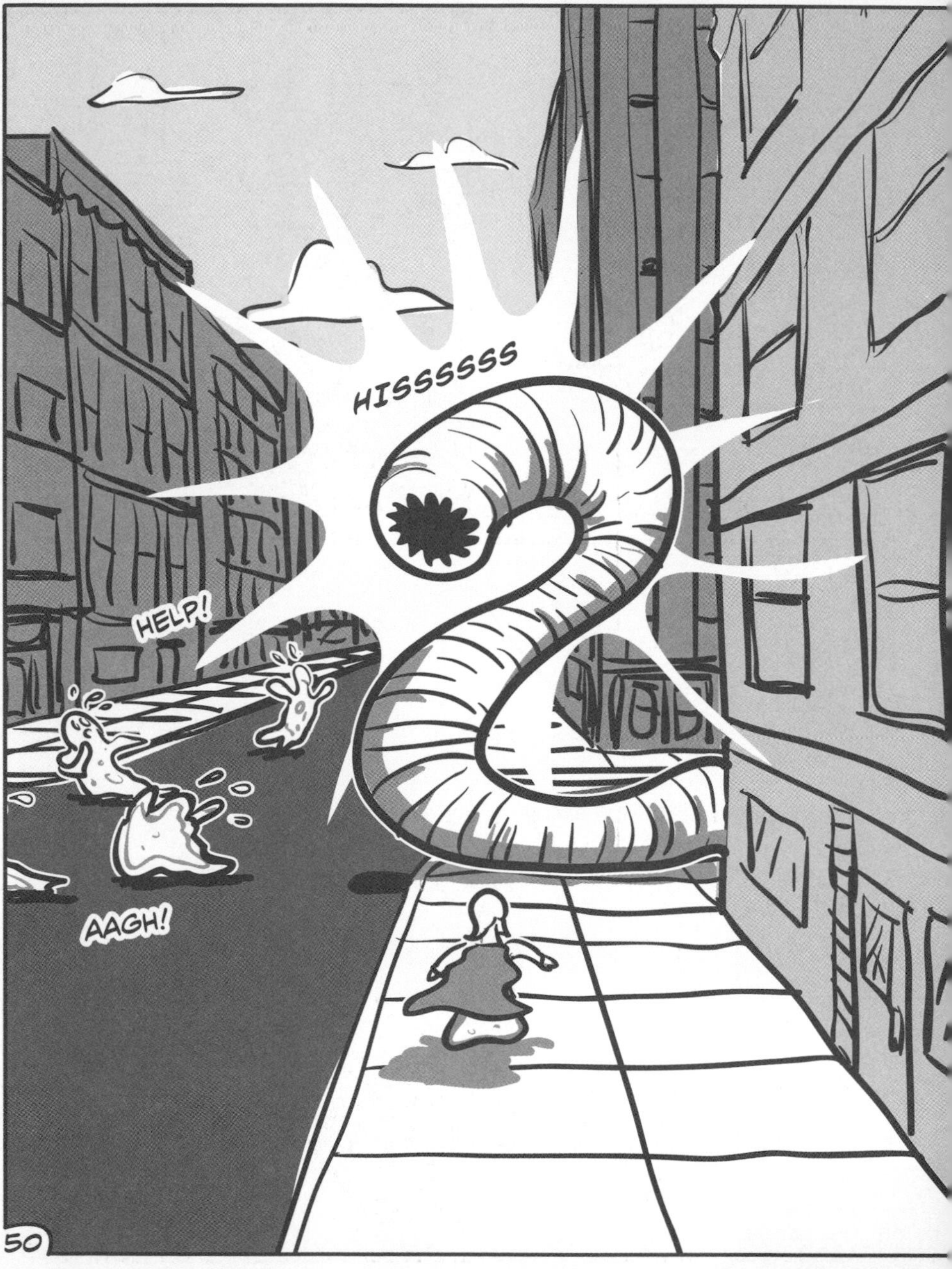
HISSSSSS
HELP!
AAGH!

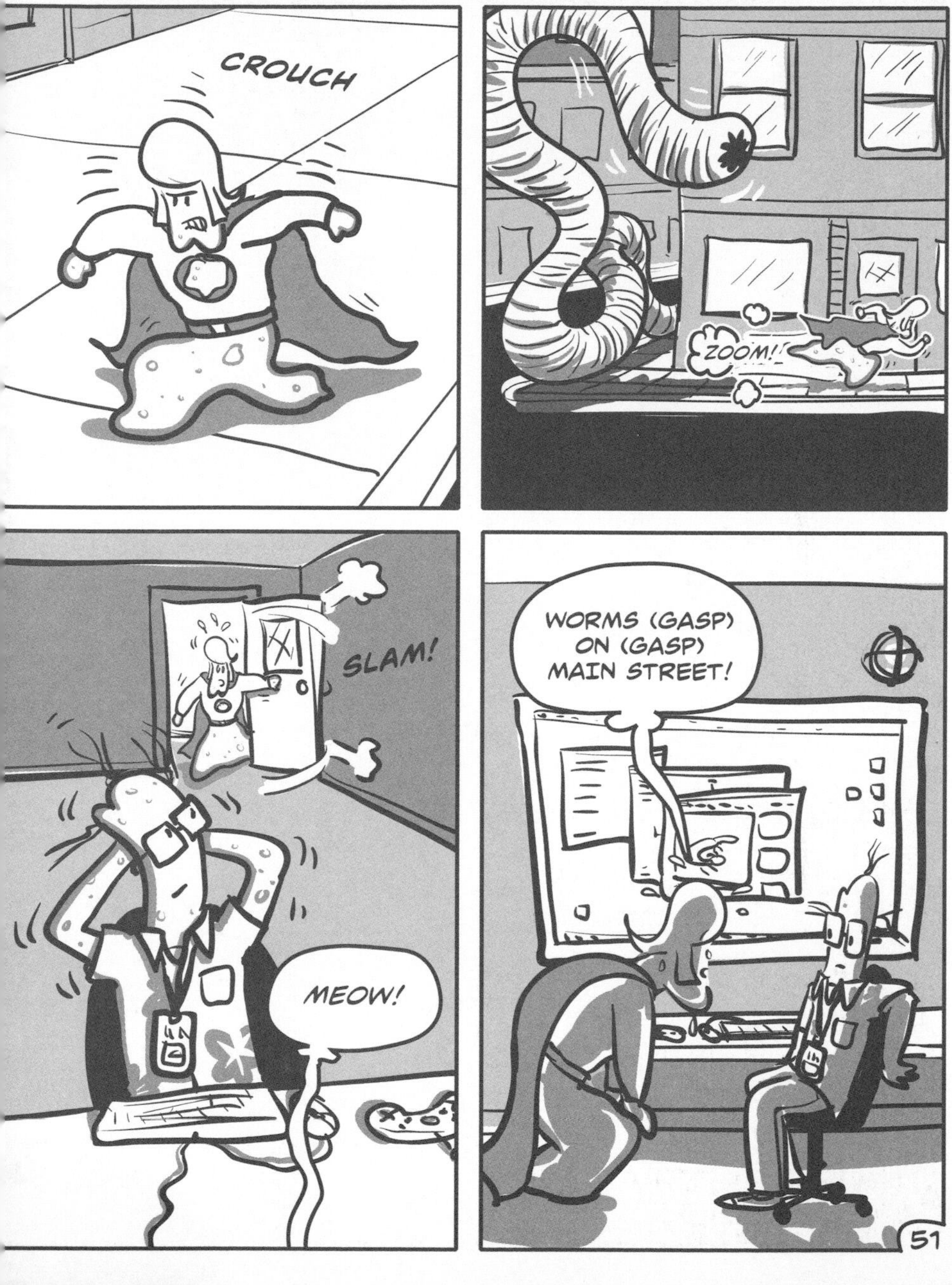
CROUCH
ZOOM!
SLAM!
MEOW!
WORMS (GASP) ON (GASP) MAIN STREET!

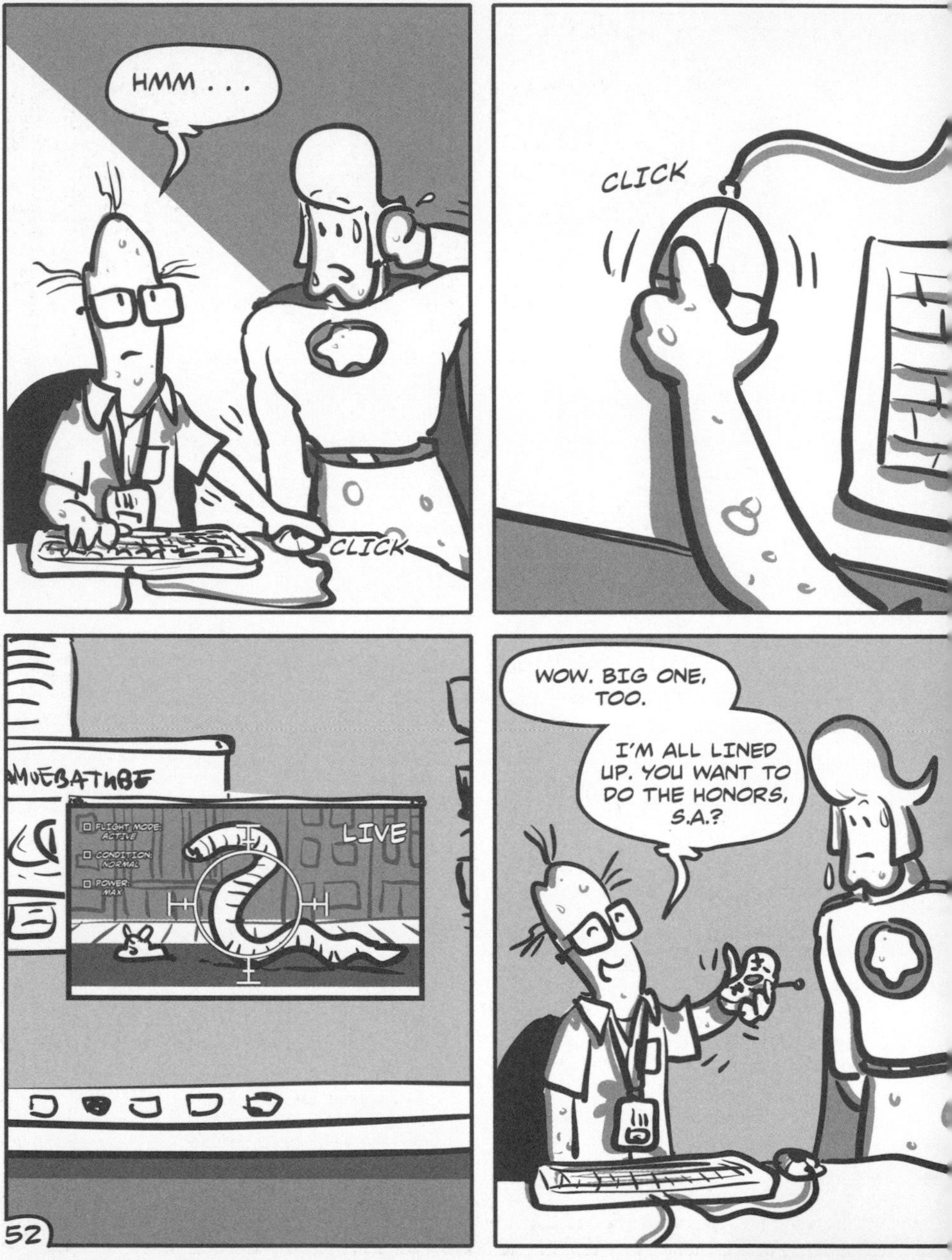
HMM . . .
CLICK
CLICK
FLIGHT MODE: ACTIVE
CONDITION: NORMAL
POWER: MAX
LIVE
WOW. BIG ONE, TOO.
I'M ALL LINED UP. YOU WANT TO DO THE HONORS, S.A.?

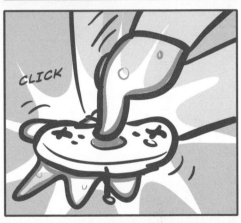

CLICK

AMOEBATUBE

FLIGHT MODE:
ACTIVE

CONDITION:
NORMAL

POWER:
MAX

LIVE

ZAP!

SIZZLE!

53

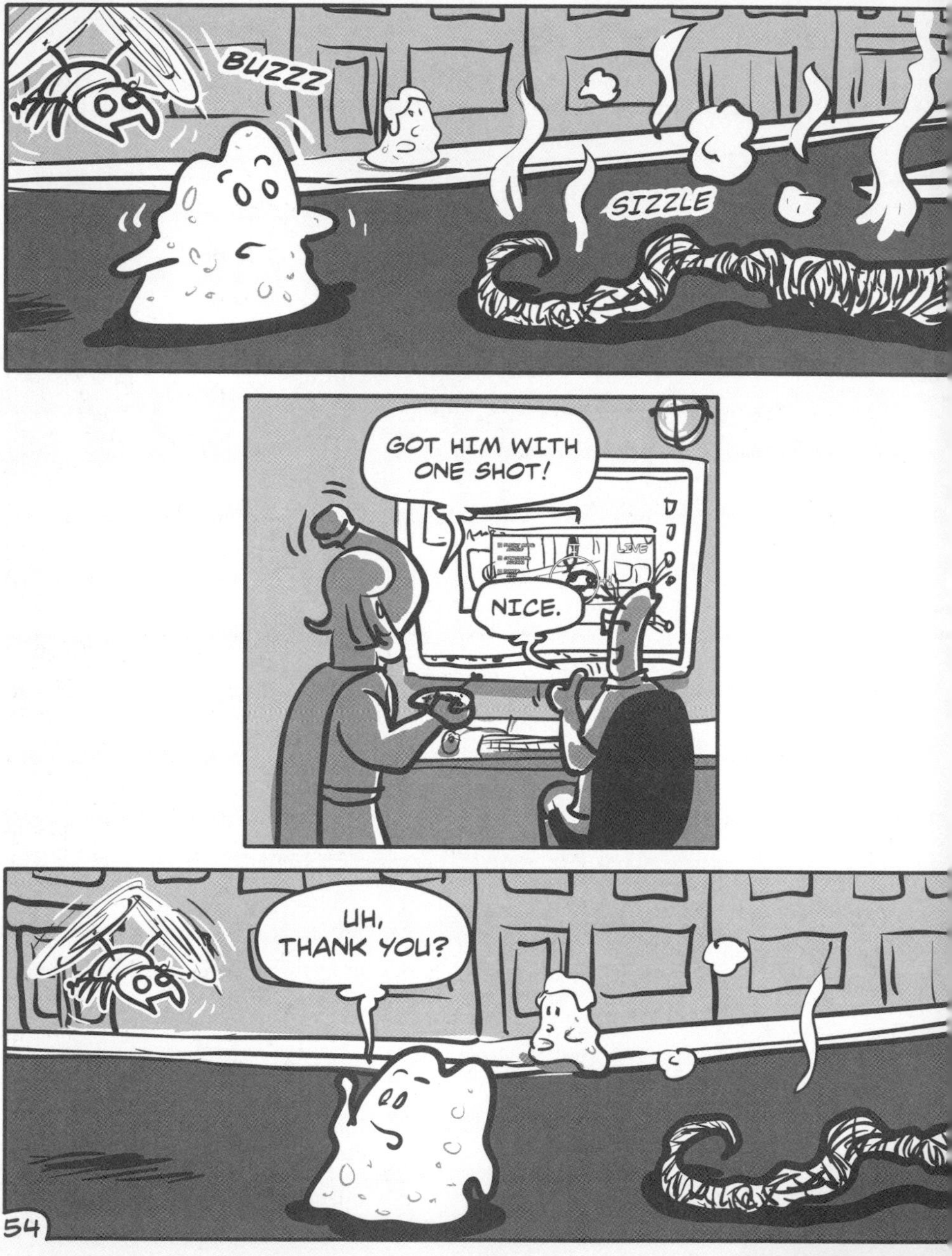
BUZZZ
SIZZLE
GOT HIM WITH ONE SHOT!
LIVE
NICE.
UH, THANK YOU?

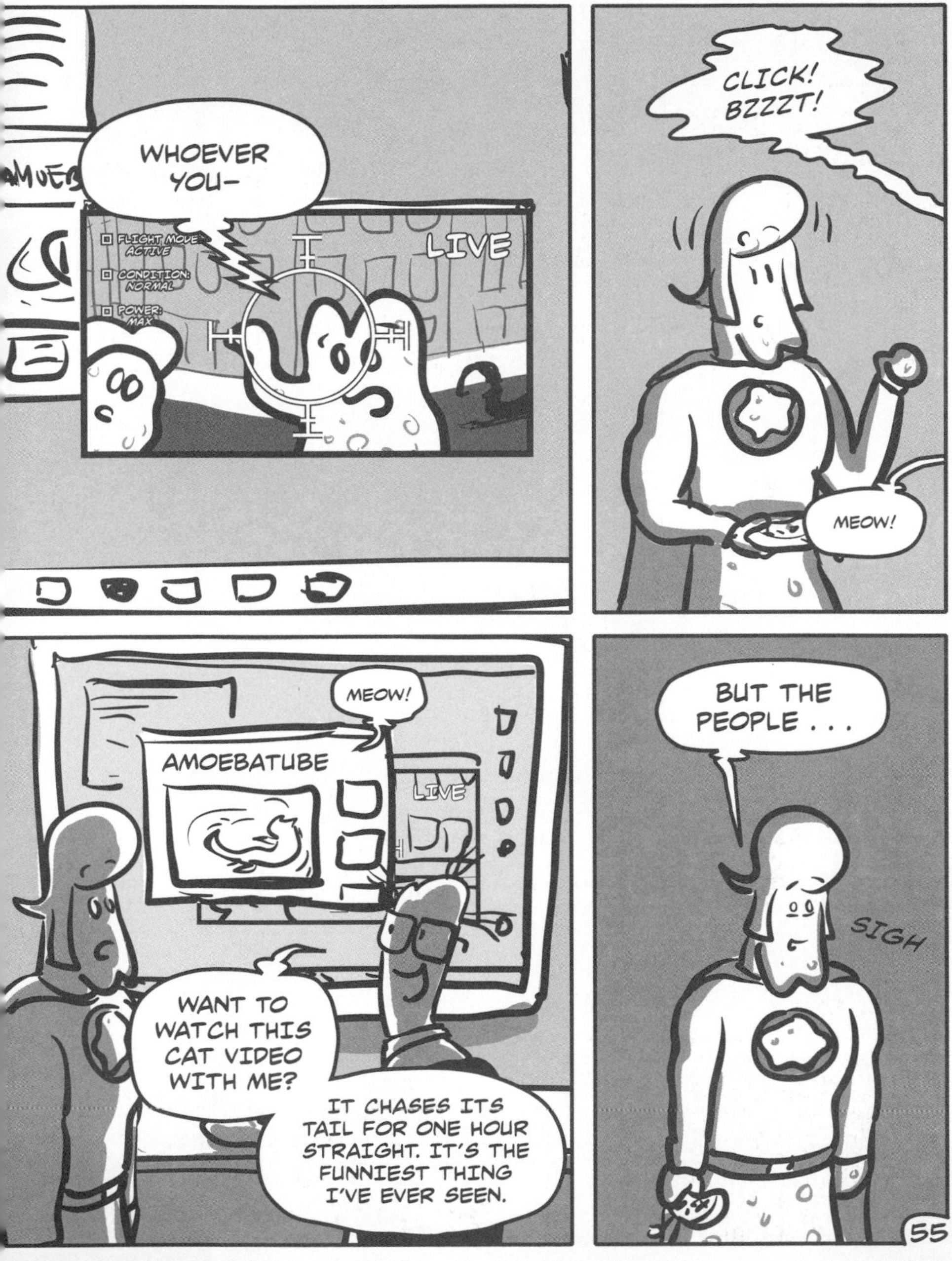
WHOEVER YOU-
FLIGHT MODE: ACTIVE
CONDITION: NORMAL
POWER: MAX
LIVE
CLICK! BZZZT!
MEOW!
MEOW!
AMOEBATUBE
LIVE
WANT TO WATCH THIS CAT VIDEO WITH ME?
IT CHASES ITS TAIL FOR ONE HOUR STRAIGHT. IT'S THE FUNNIEST THING I'VE EVER SEEN.
BUT THE PEOPLE . . .
SIGH

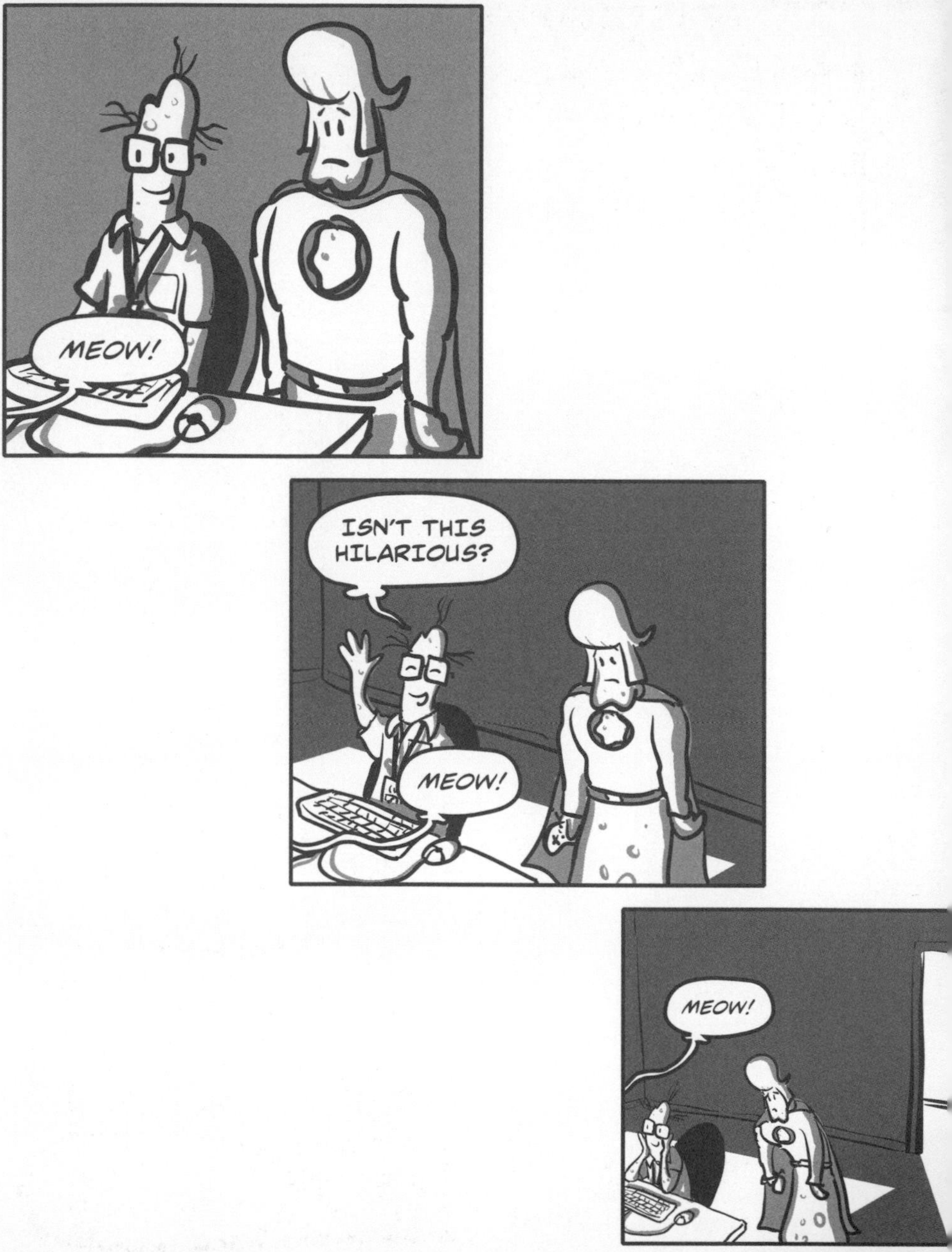
MEOW!
ISN'T THIS HILARIOUS?
MEOW!
MEOW!

Dad, can I talk to you about something?

Sure, Squish! You can talk to me about anything!

Pod's been acting really strange lately. Well, stranger than usual.

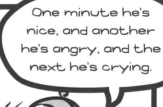

One minute he's nice, and another he's angry, and the next he's crying.

I don't know what's going on!

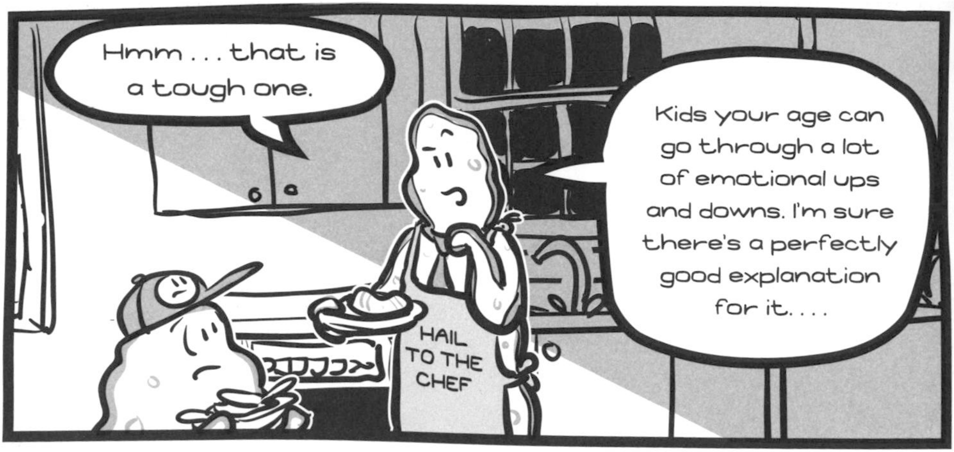
Hmm . . . that is a tough one.
Kids your age can go through a lot of emotional ups and downs. I'm sure there's a perfectly good explanation for it. . . .
HAIL TO THE CHEF

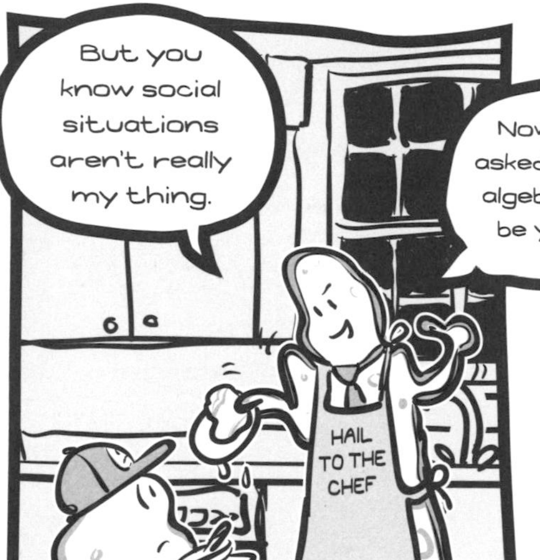
But you know social situations aren't really my thing.
Now, if you'd asked me about algebra, I would be your guy.
HAIL TO THE CHEF

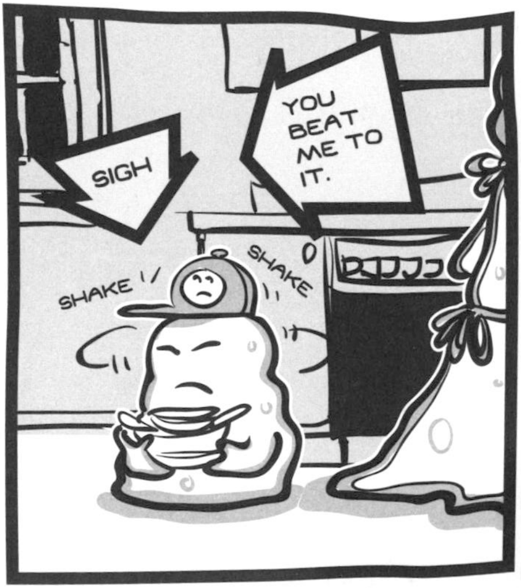
SIGH
YOU BEAT ME TO IT.
SHAKE
SHAKE

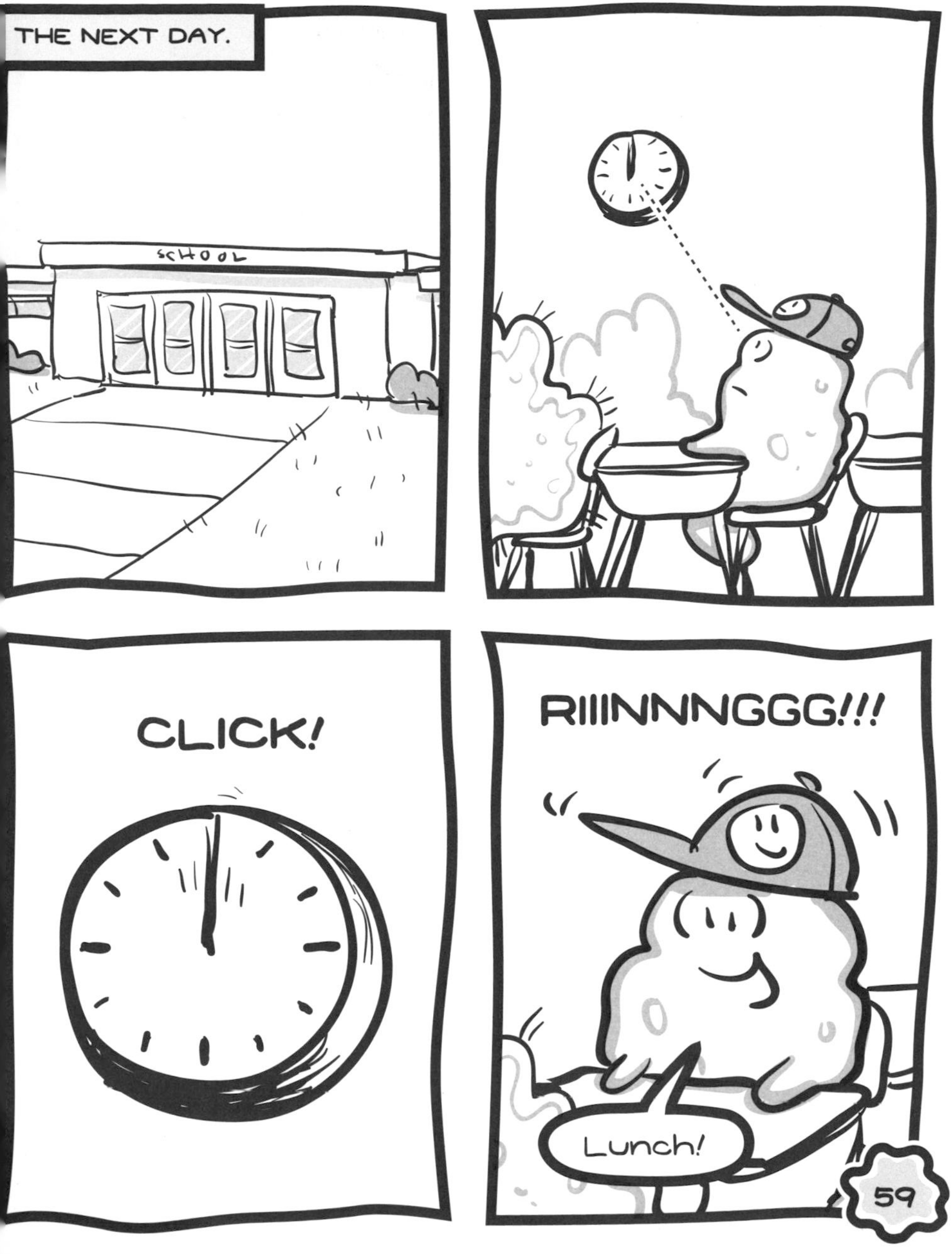
THE NEXT DAY.
SCHOOL
CLICK!
RIIINNNGGG!!!
Lunch!

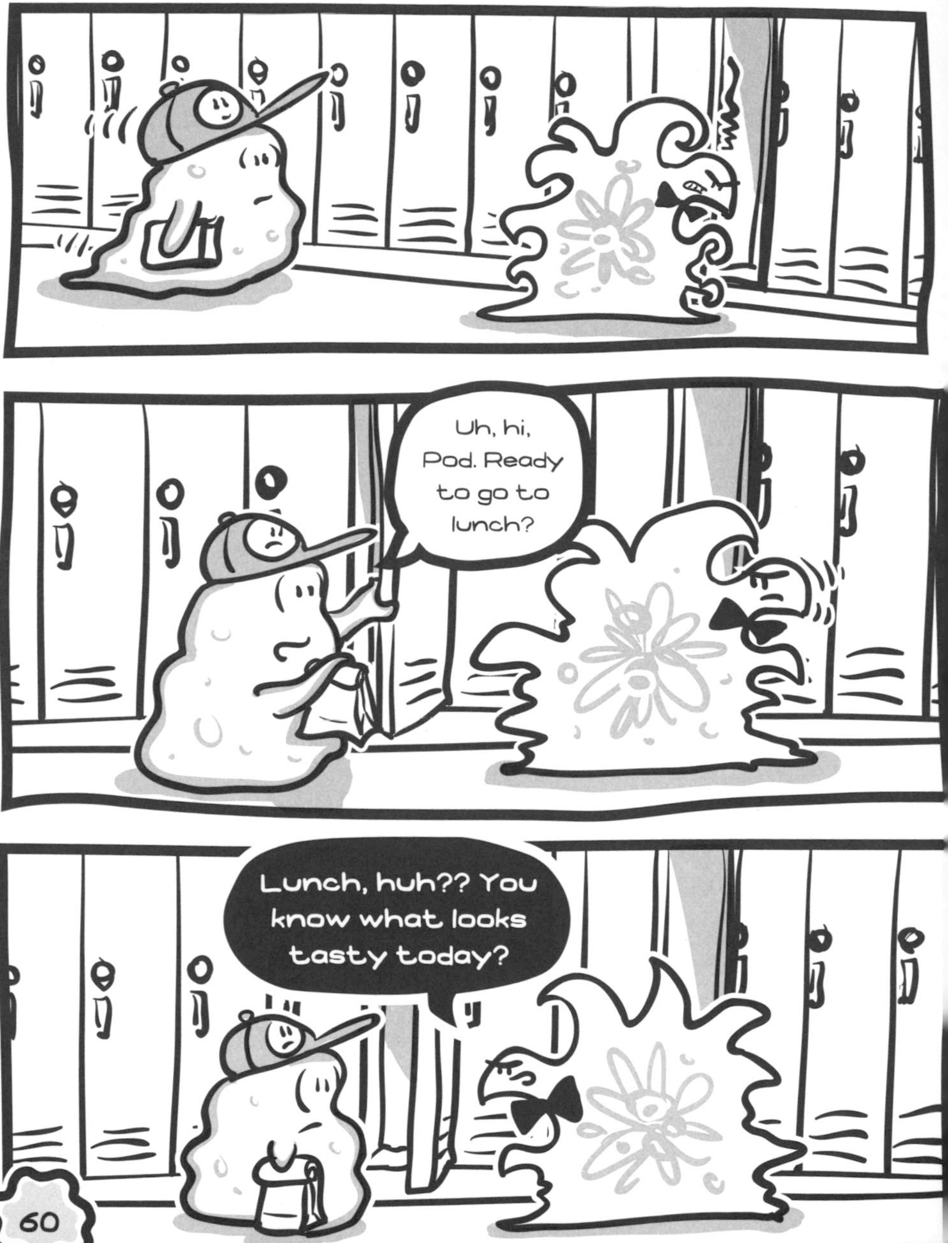
Uh, hi, Pod. Ready to go to lunch?
Lunch, huh?? You know what looks tasty today?

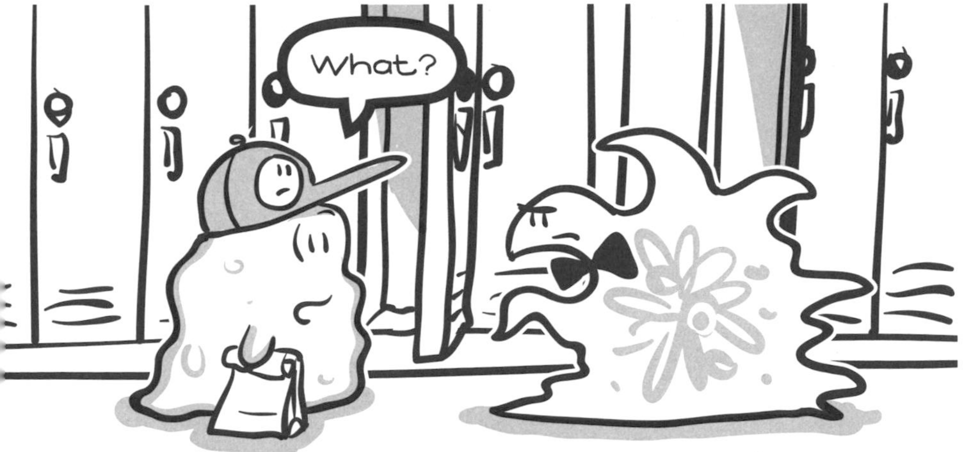
What?

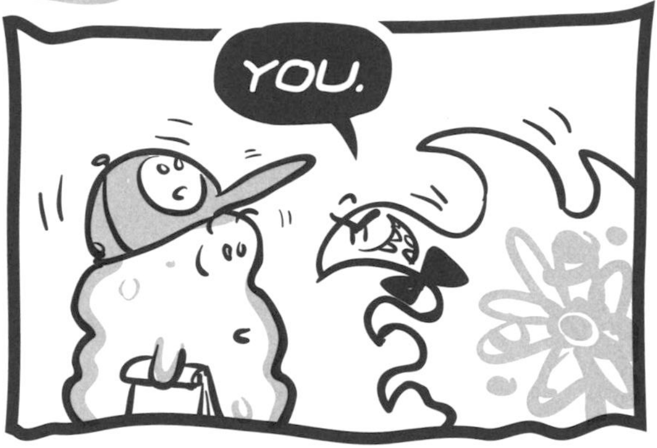
YOU.

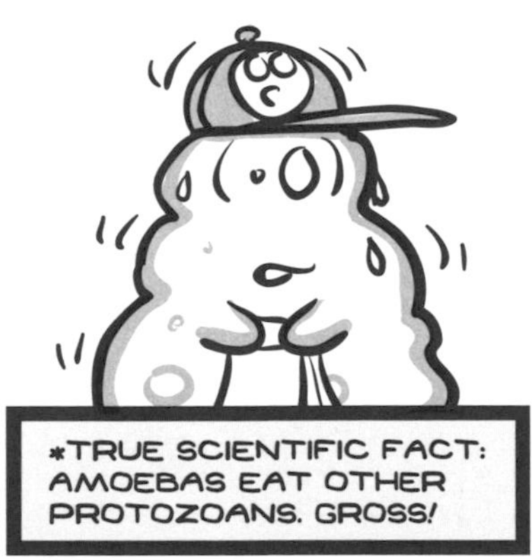
*TRUE SCIENTIFIC FACT:
AMOEBAS EAT OTHER
PROTOZOANS. GROSS!

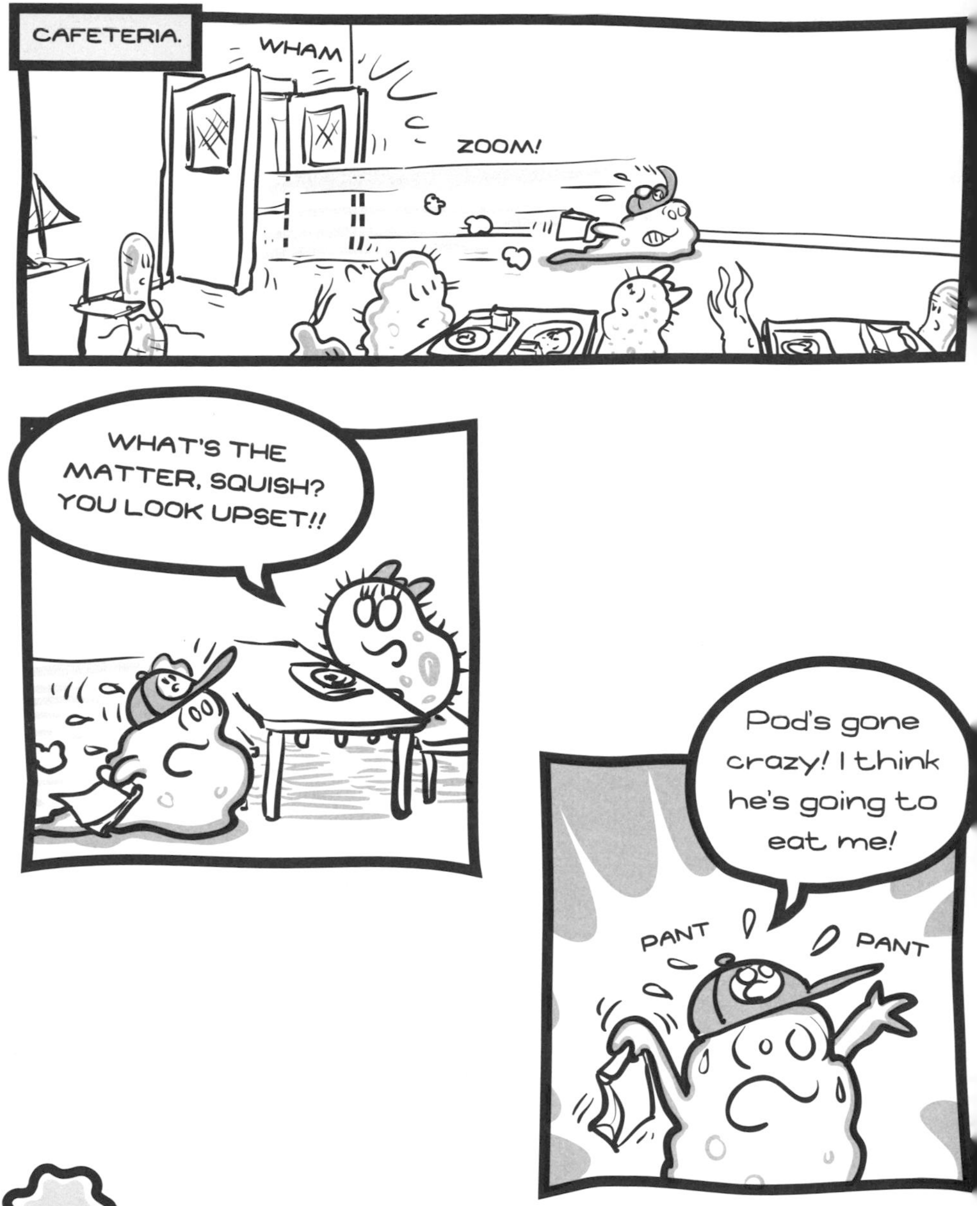
CAFETERIA.
WHAM
ZOOM!
WHAT'S THE MATTER, SQUISH? YOU LOOK UPSET!!
Pod's gone crazy! I think he's going to eat me!
PANT
PANT

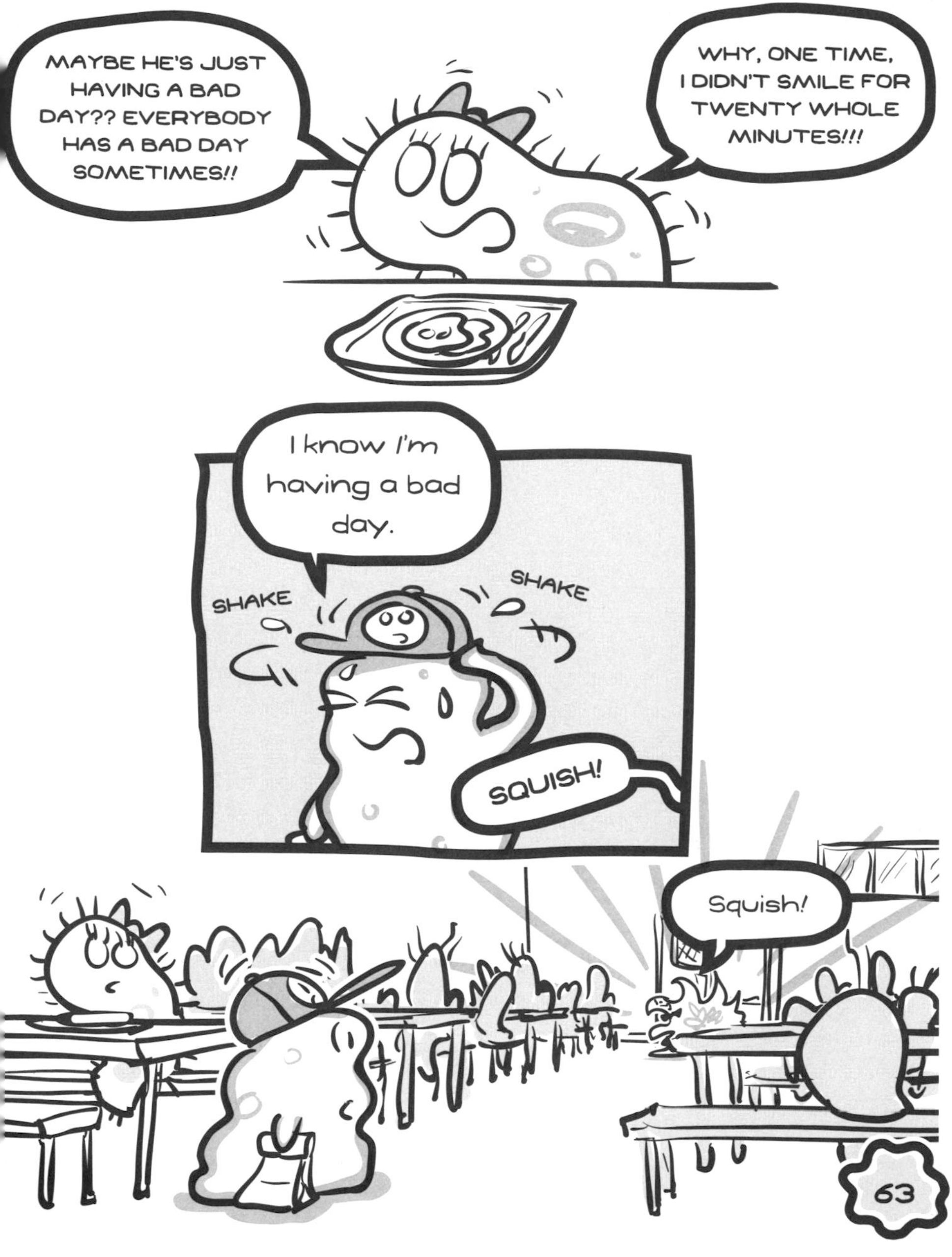
MAYBE HE'S JUST HAVING A BAD DAY?? EVERYBODY HAS A BAD DAY SOMETIMES!!
WHY, ONE TIME, I DIDN'T SMILE FOR TWENTY WHOLE MINUTES!!!
I know I'm having a bad day.
SHAKE
SHAKE
SQUISH!
Squish!

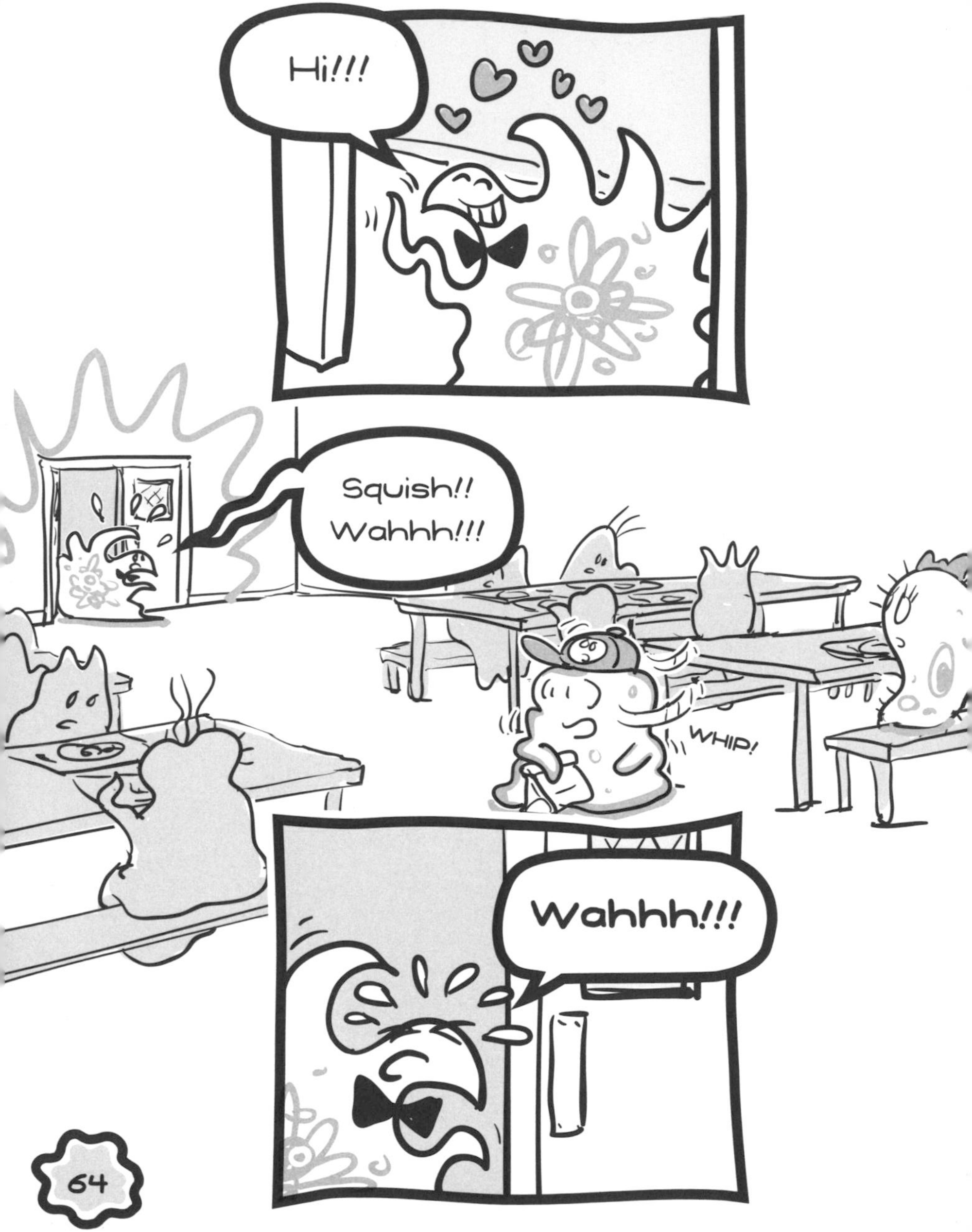
Hi!!!
Squish!! Wahhh!!!
WHIP!
Wahhh!!!

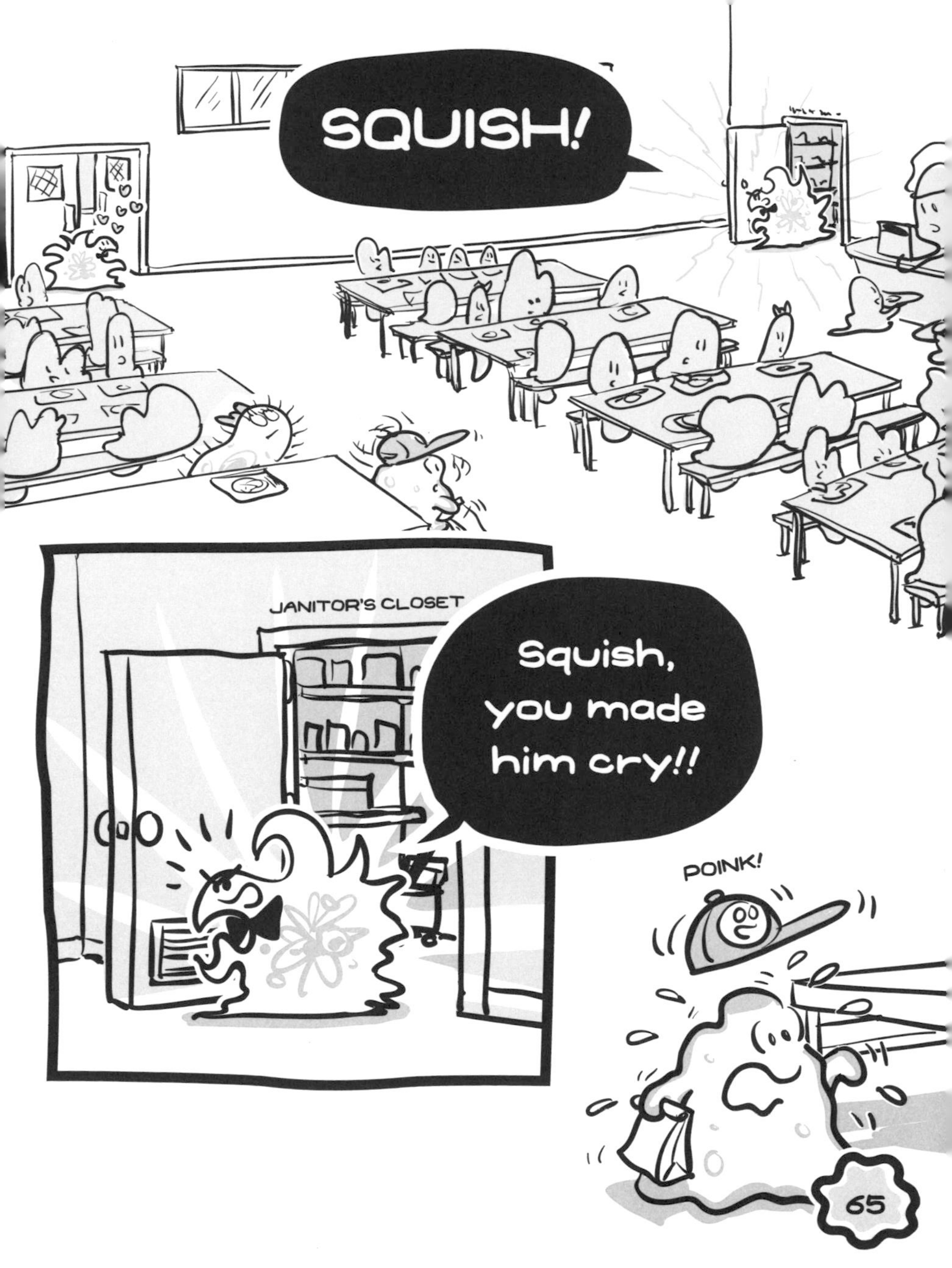
SQUISH!
JANITOR'S CLOSET
Squish, you made him cry!!
POINK!

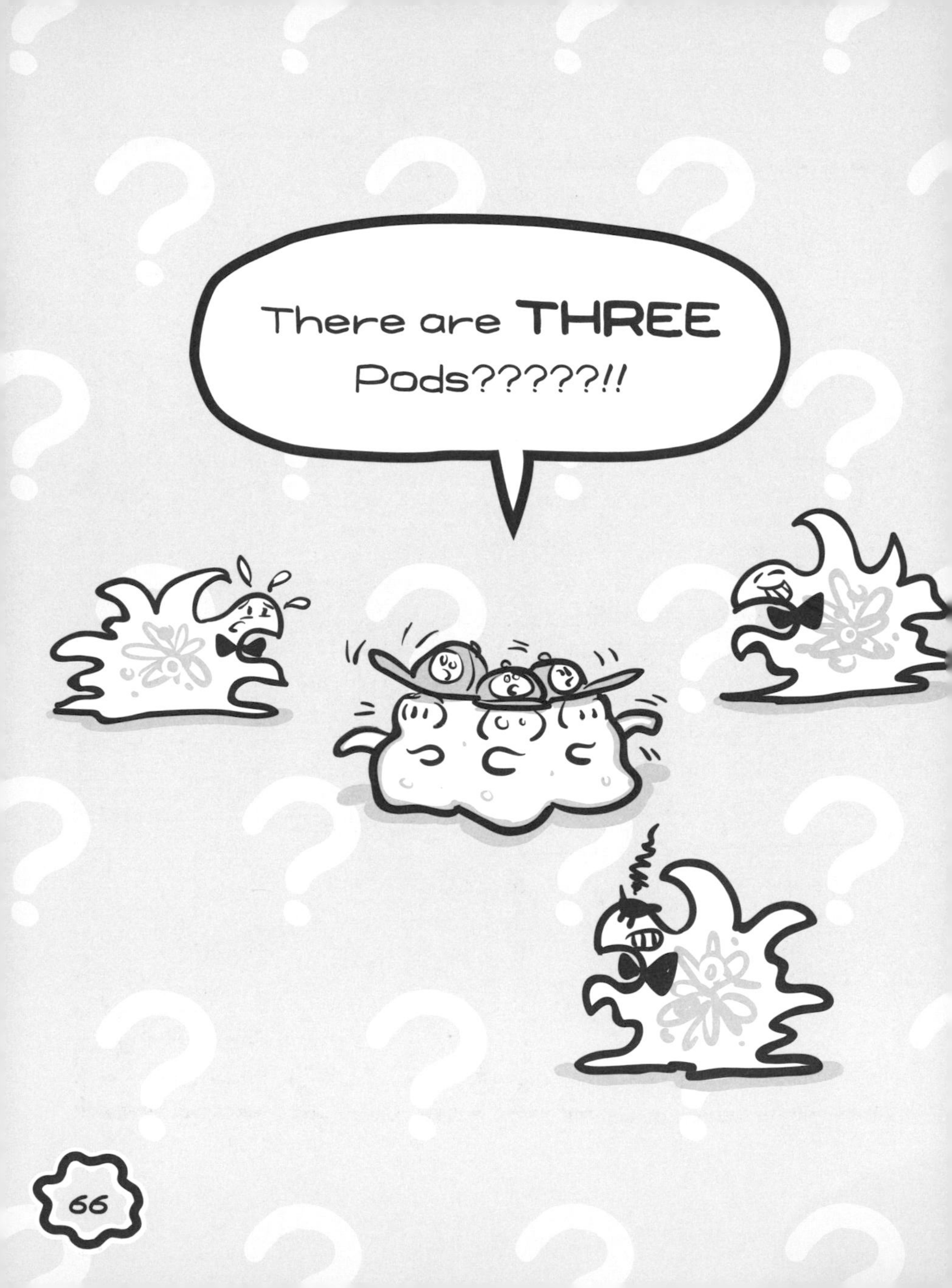
There are THREE Pods??????!!

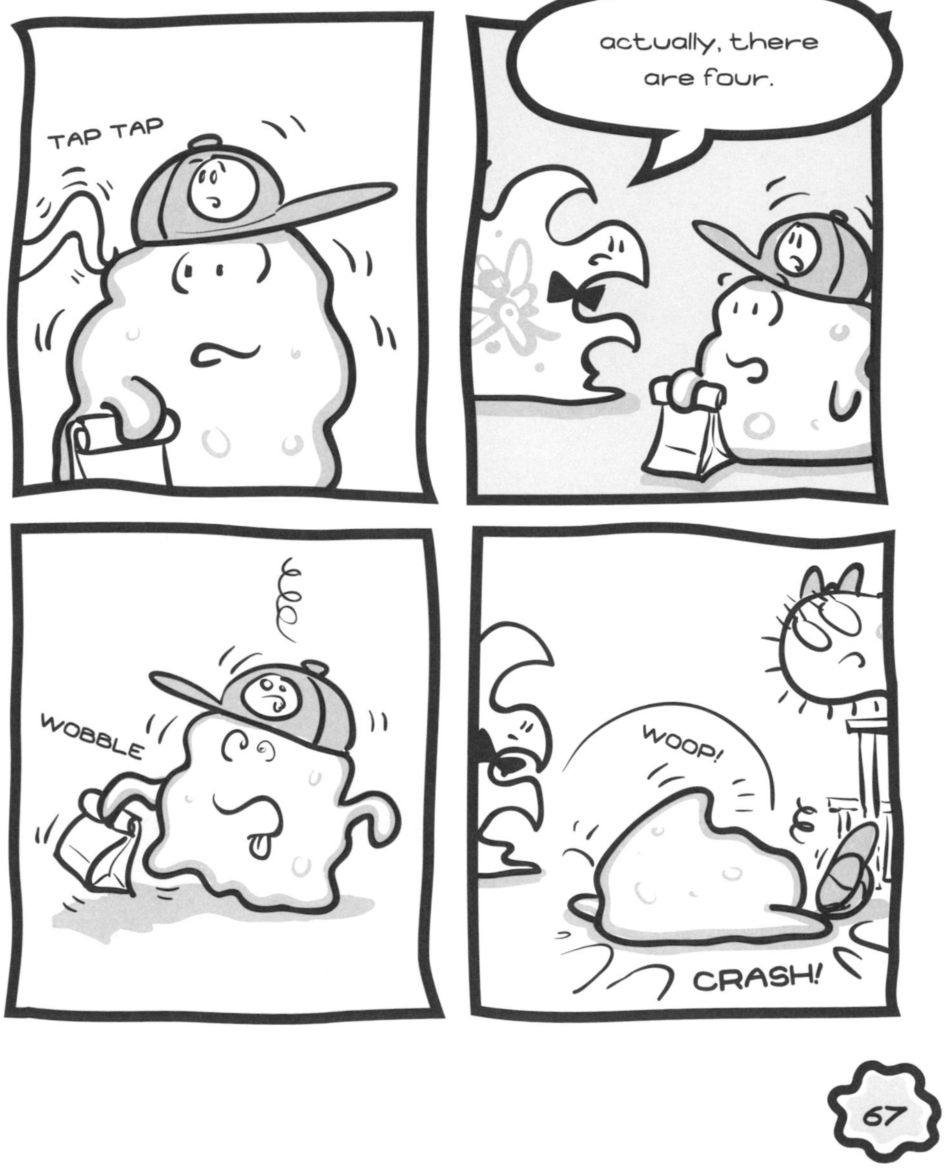
TAP TAP
actually, there are four.
WOBBLE
WOOP!
CRASH!

i guess he
won't be eating
his lunch.

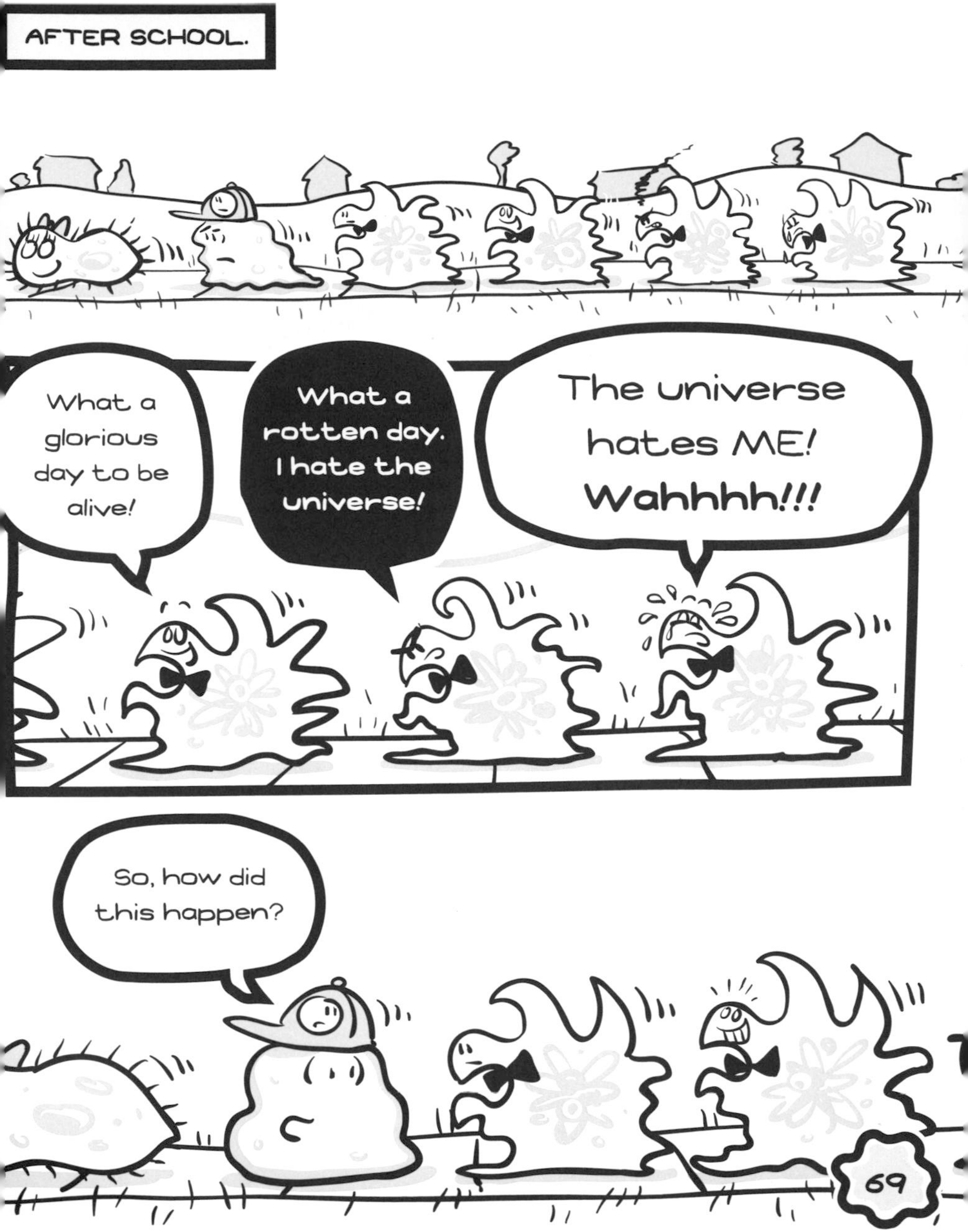
AFTER SCHOOL.
What a glorious day to be alive!
What a rotten day. I hate the universe!
The universe hates ME! Wahhhh!!!
So, how did this happen?

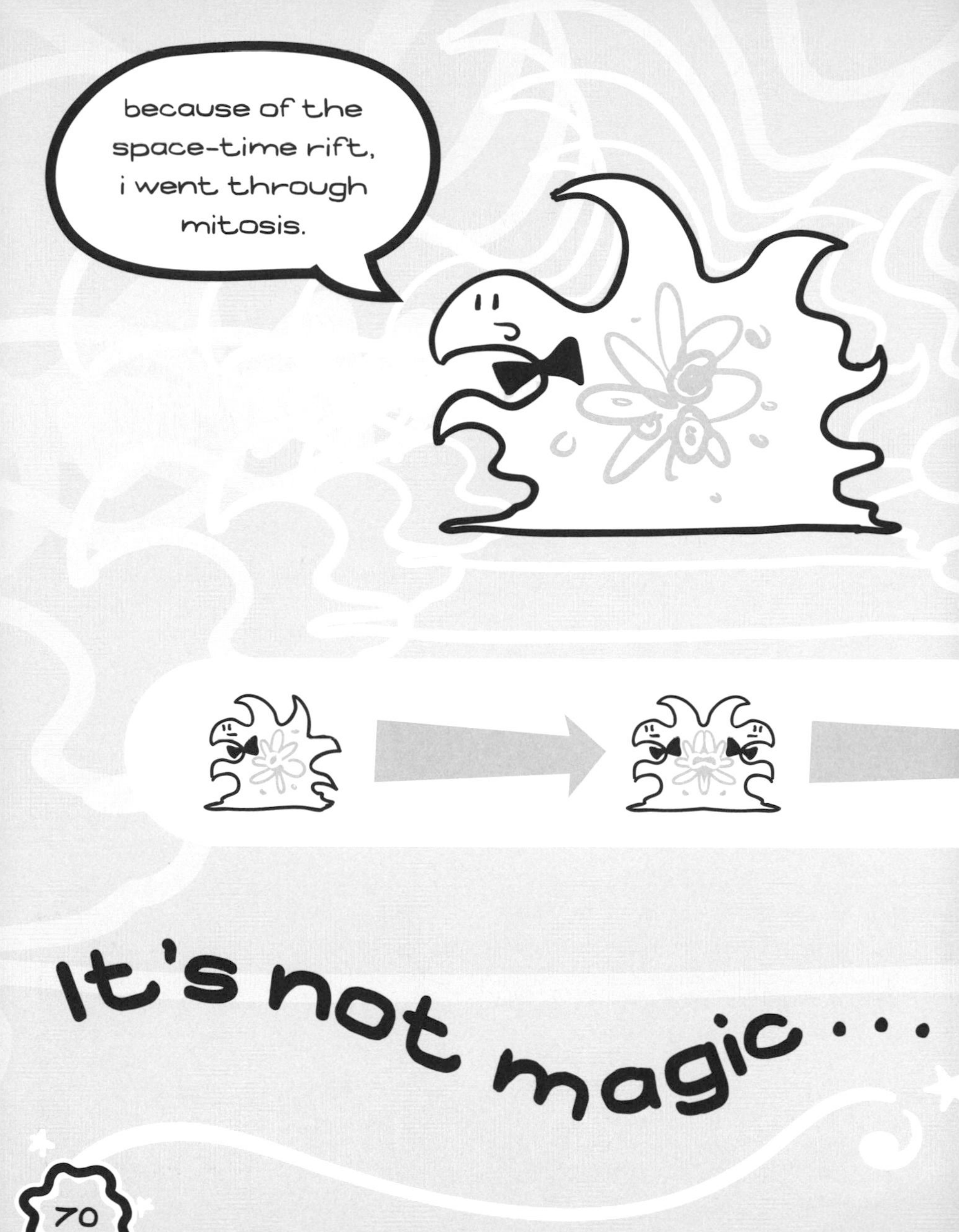

because of the space-time rift, i went through mitosis.
It's not magic...

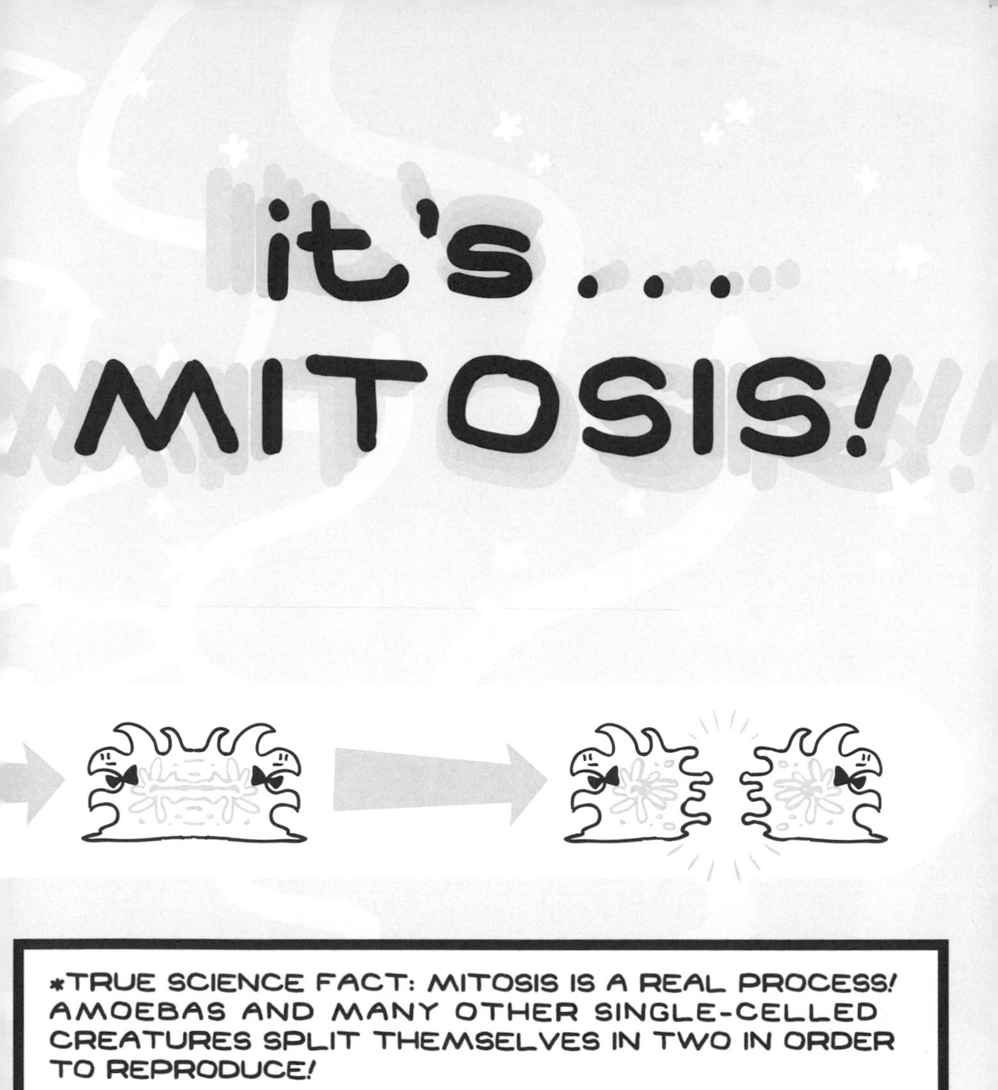
it's...
MITOSIS!

*TRUE SCIENCE FACT: MITOSIS IS A REAL PROCESS! AMOEBAS AND MANY OTHER SINGLE-CELLED CREATURES SPLIT THEMSELVES IN TWO IN ORDER TO REPRODUCE!

**THEY USUALLY DON'T NEED A SPACE-TIME RIFT, THOUGH.

***WHAT GOOD IS A COMIC BOOK WITHOUT A SPACE-TIME RIFT?

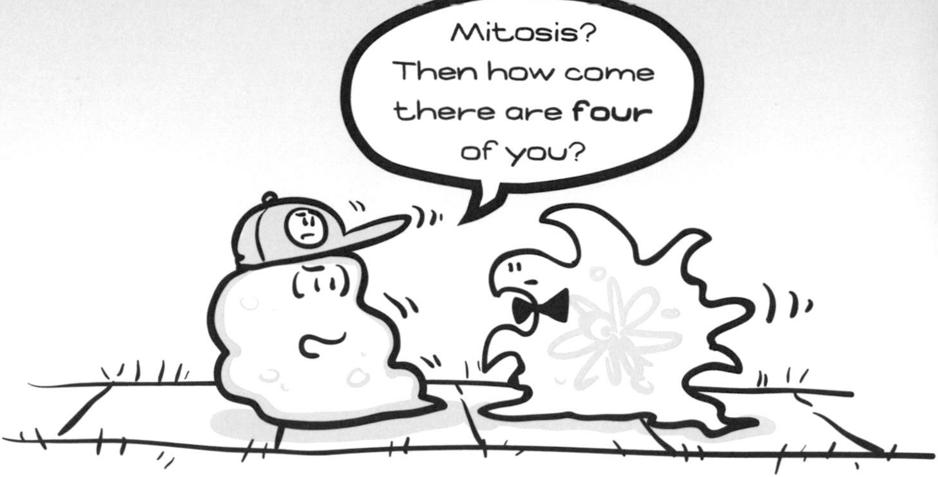
Mitosis? Then how come there are **four** of you?

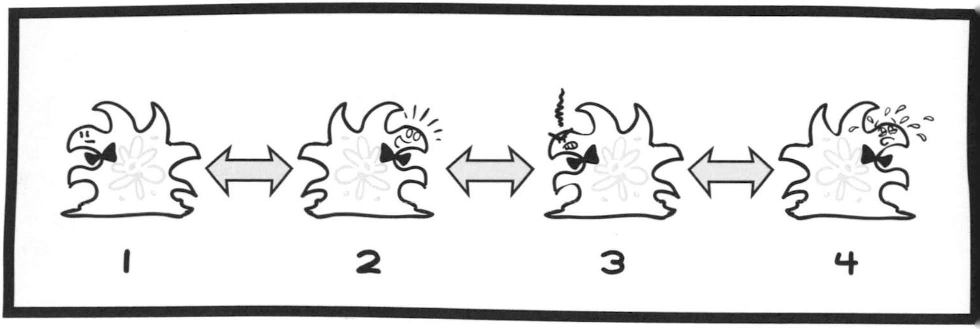
1
2
3
4

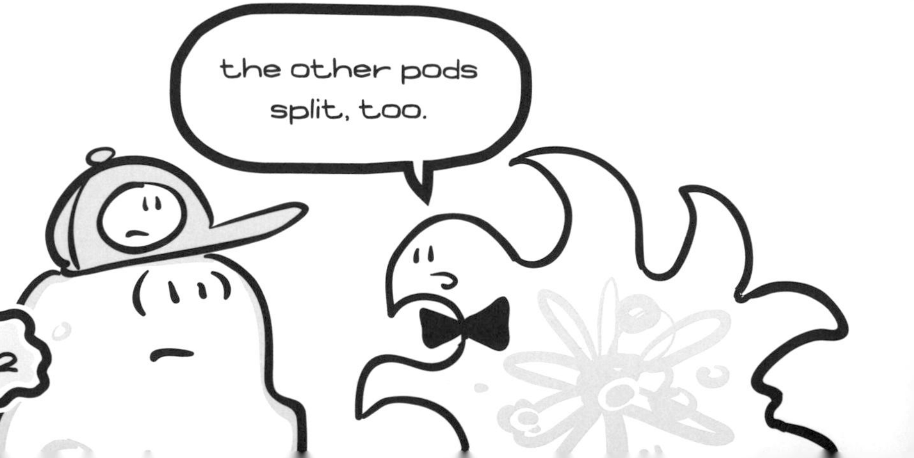
the other pods split, too.

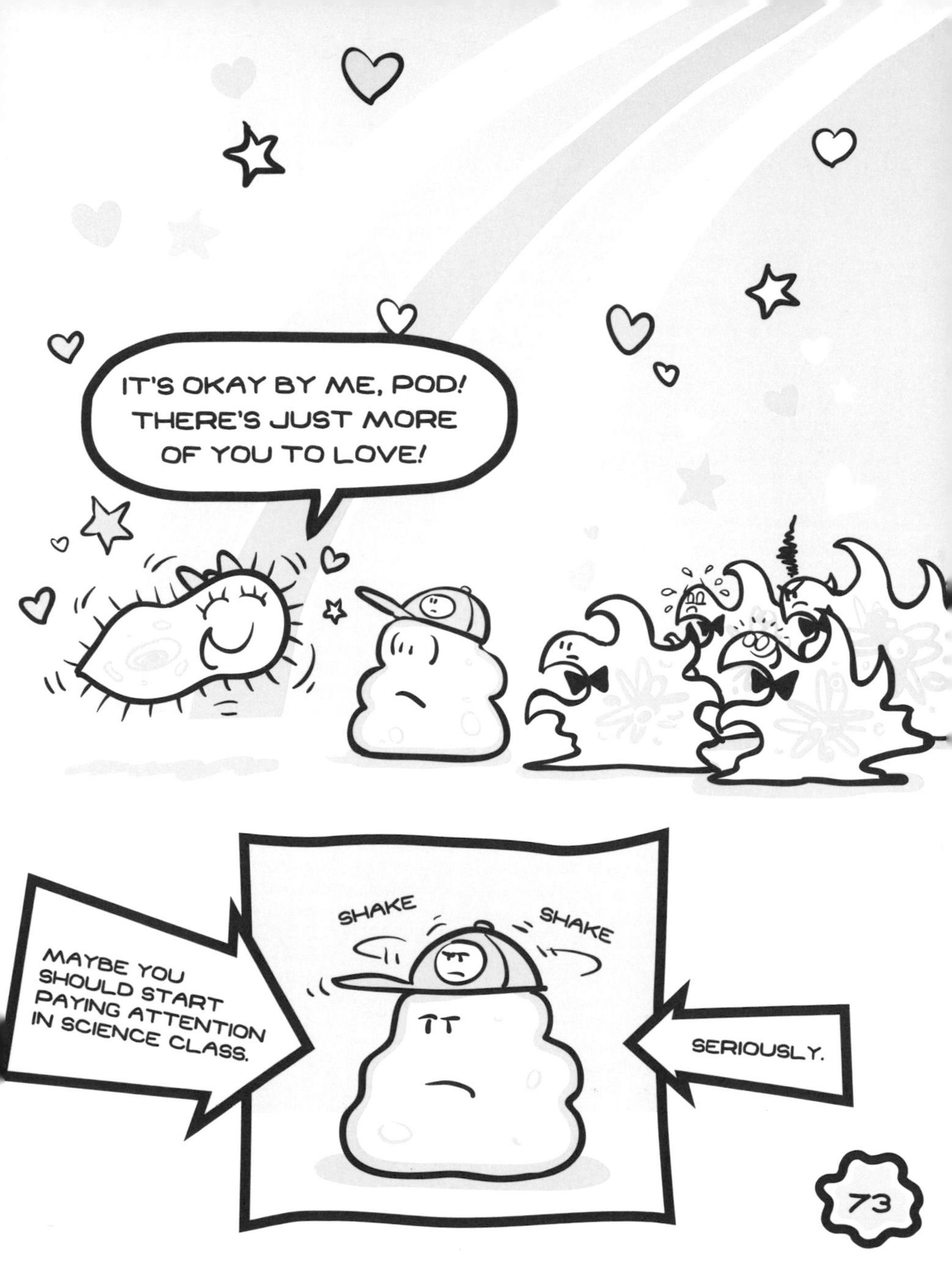
IT'S OKAY BY ME, POD! THERE'S JUST MORE OF YOU TO LOVE!
SHAKE
SHAKE
MAYBE YOU SHOULD START PAYING ATTENTION IN SCIENCE CLASS.
SERIOUSLY.

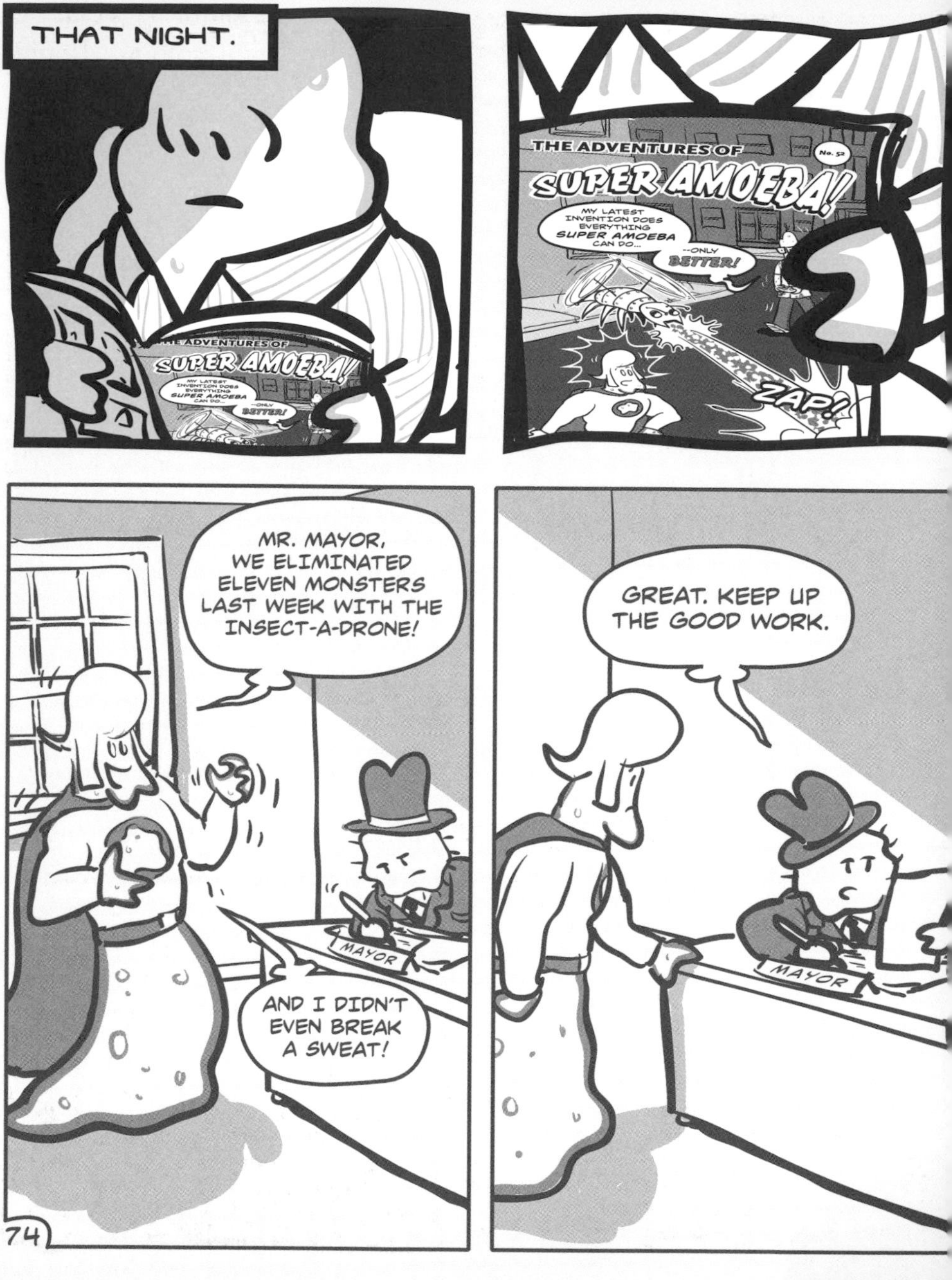
THAT NIGHT.
THE ADVENTURES OF
SUPER AMOEBA!
No. 52
MY LATEST INVENTION DOES EVERYTHING SUPER AMOEBA CAN DO...
--ONLY BETTER!
ZAP!
MR. MAYOR, WE ELIMINATED ELEVEN MONSTERS LAST WEEK WITH THE INSECT-A-DRONE!
AND I DIDN'T EVEN BREAK A SWEAT!
MAYOR
GREAT. KEEP UP THE GOOD WORK.
MAYOR

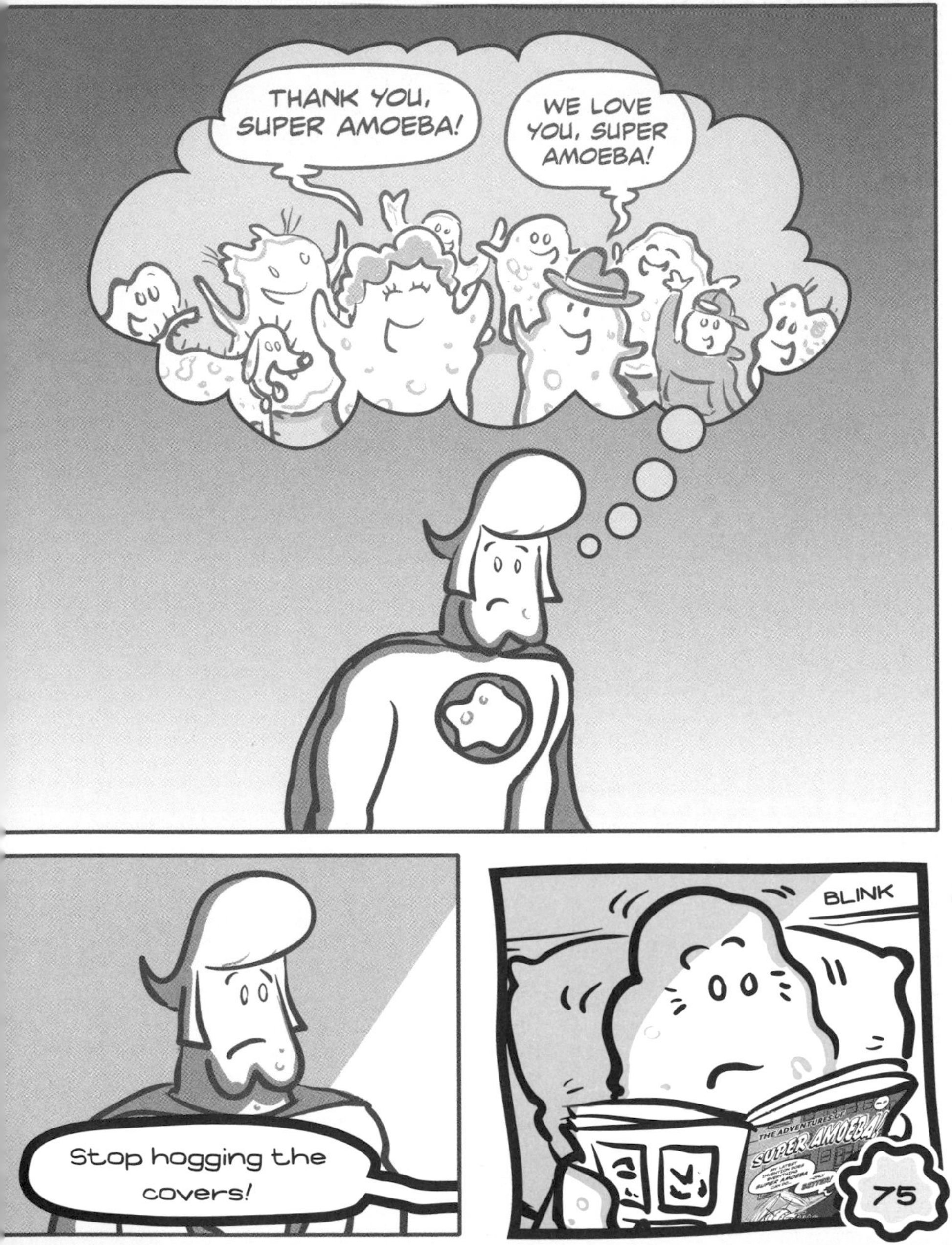
THANK YOU, SUPER AMOEBA!
WE LOVE YOU, SUPER AMOEBA!
Stop hogging the covers!
BLINK
THE ADVENTURES OF SUPER AMOEBA!

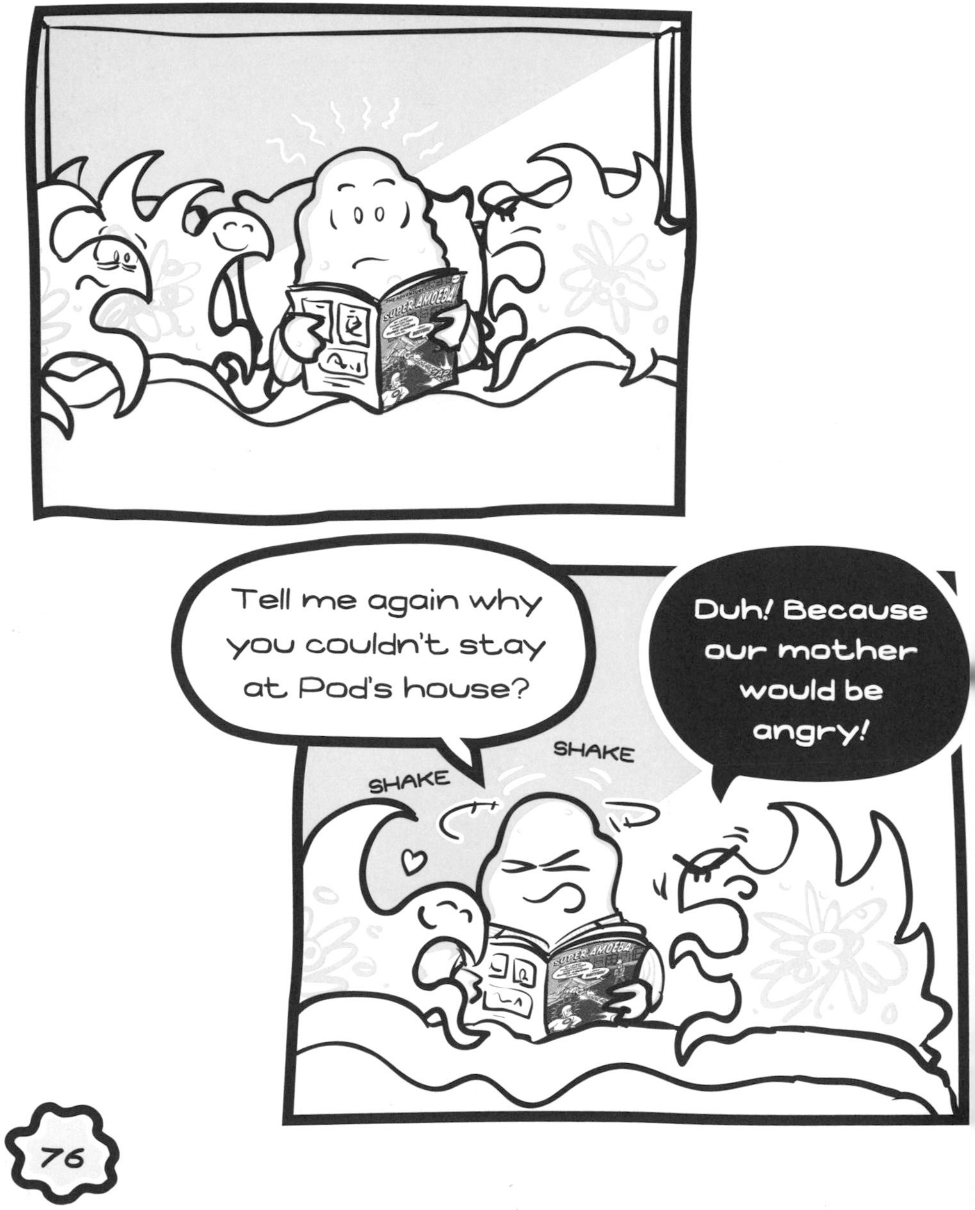
Tell me again why you couldn't stay at Pod's house?
Duh! Because our mother would be angry!
SHAKE
SHAKE

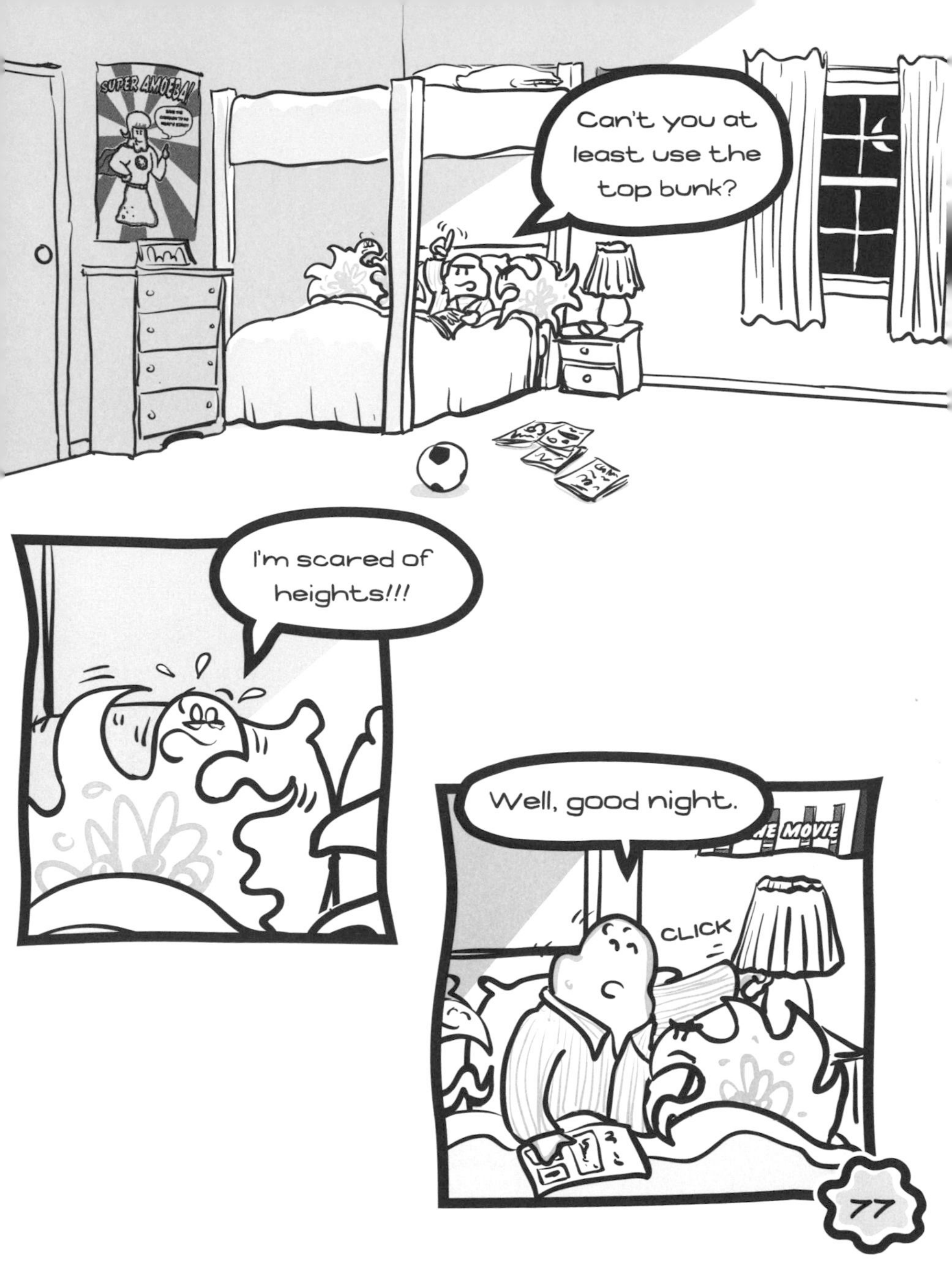
SUPER AMOEBA!
Can't you at least use the top bunk?
I'm scared of heights!!!
Well, good night.
THE MOVIE
CLICK

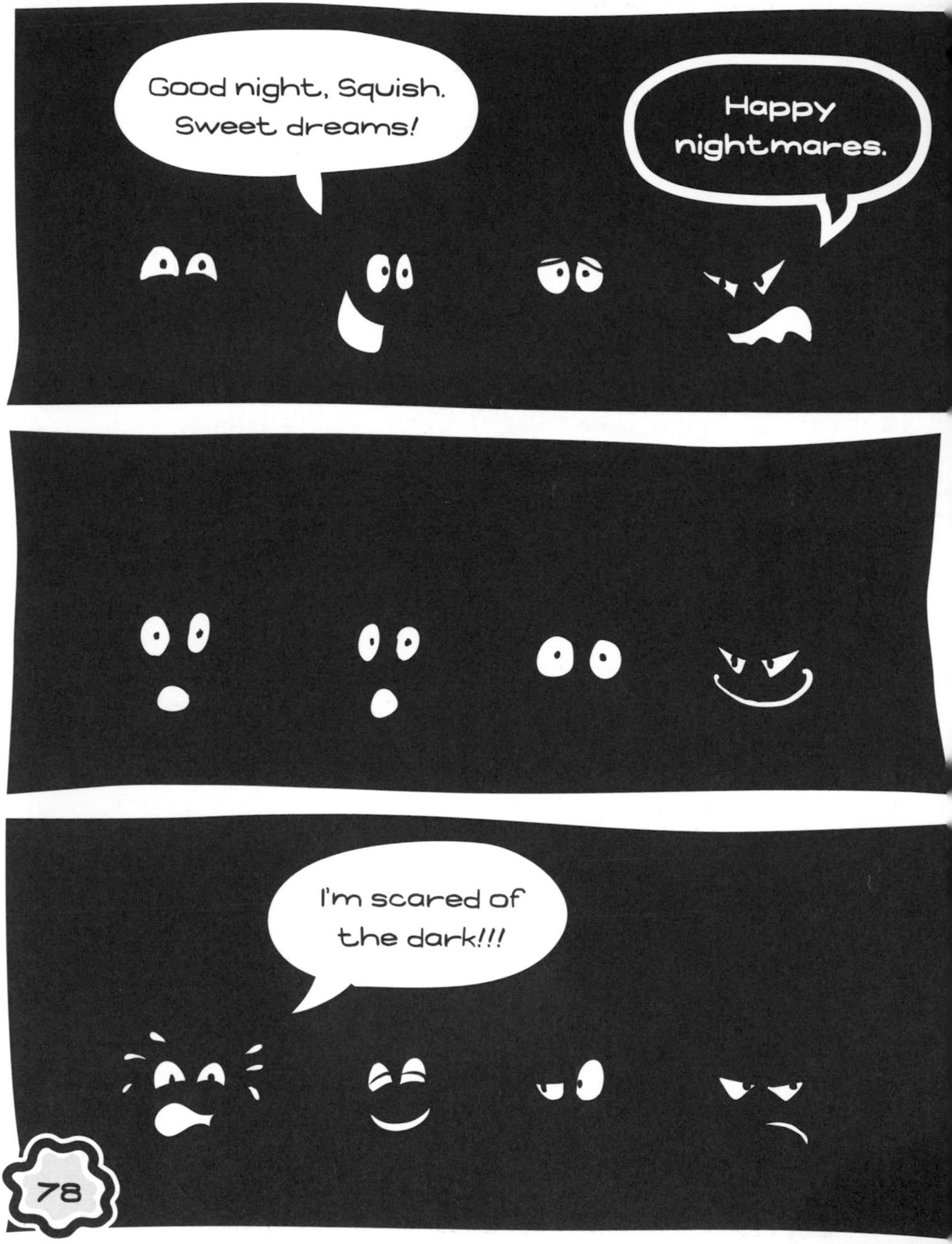
Good night, Squish. Sweet dreams!
Happy nightmares.
I'm scared of the dark!!!

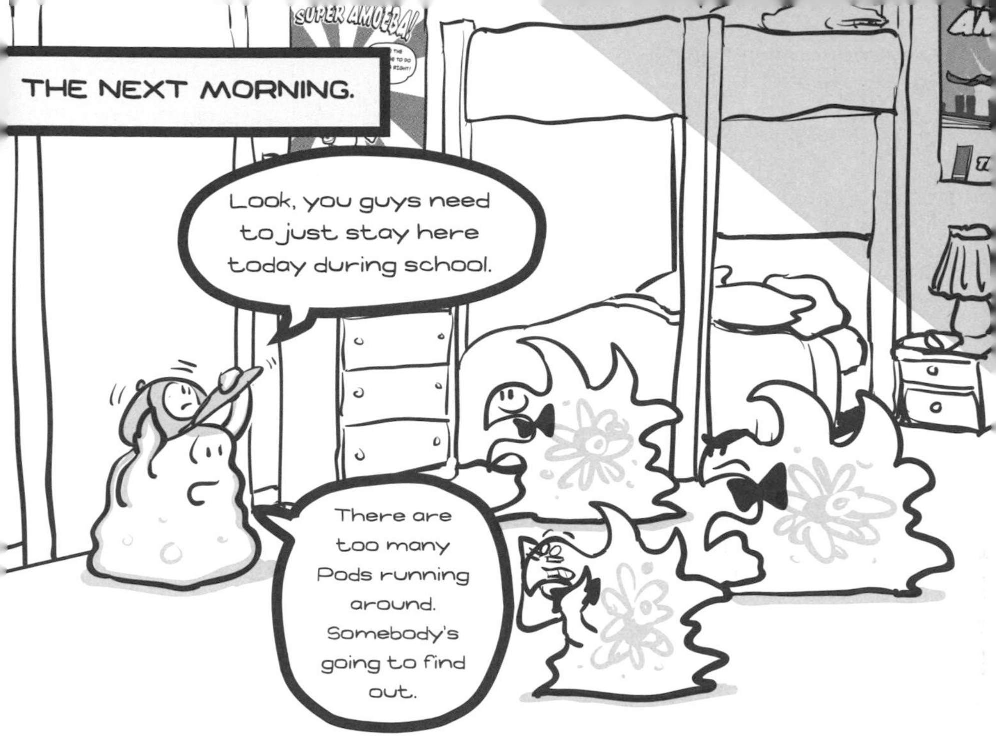
SUPER AMOEBA!
THE NEXT MORNING.
Look, you guys need to just stay here today during school.
There are too many Pods running around. Somebody's going to find out.

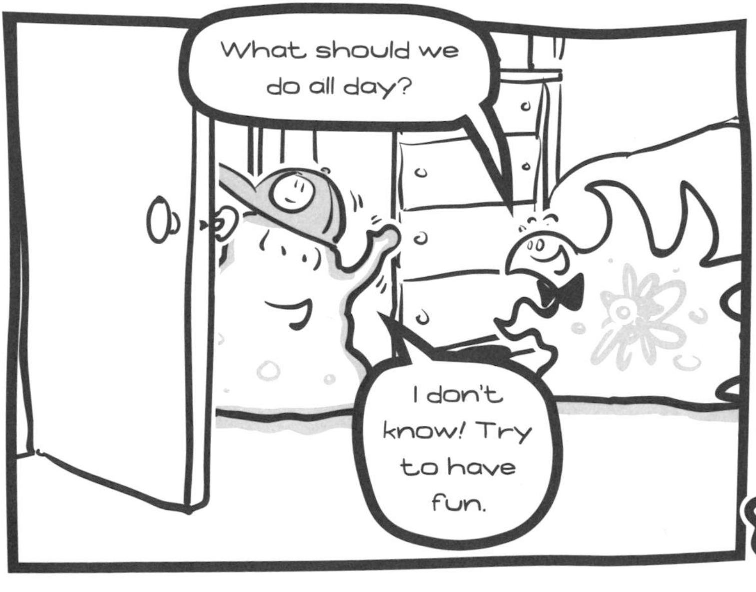
What should we do all day?
I don't know! Try to have fun.

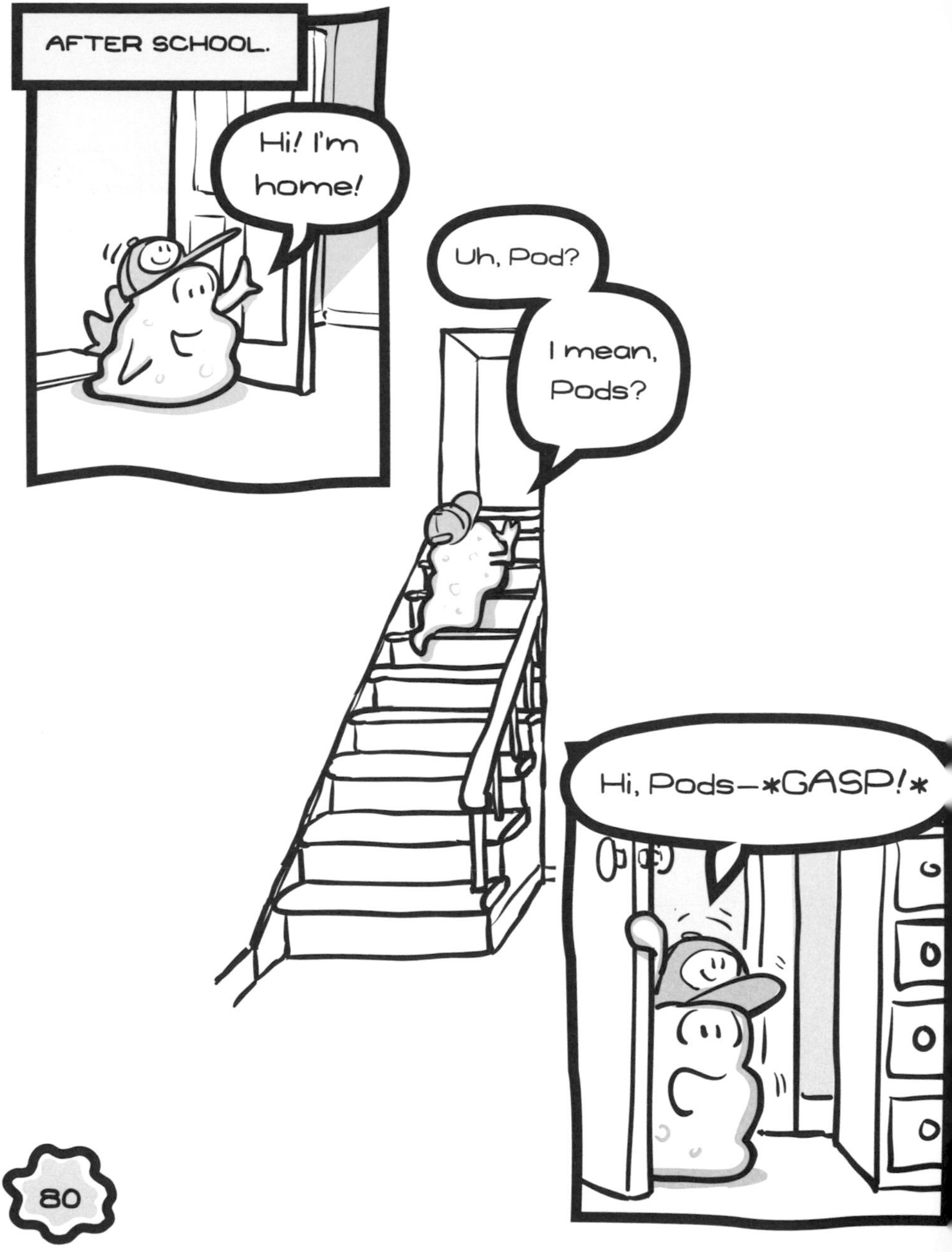
AFTER SCHOOL.
Hi! I'm home!
Uh, Pod?
I mean, Pods?
Hi, Pods—*GASP!*

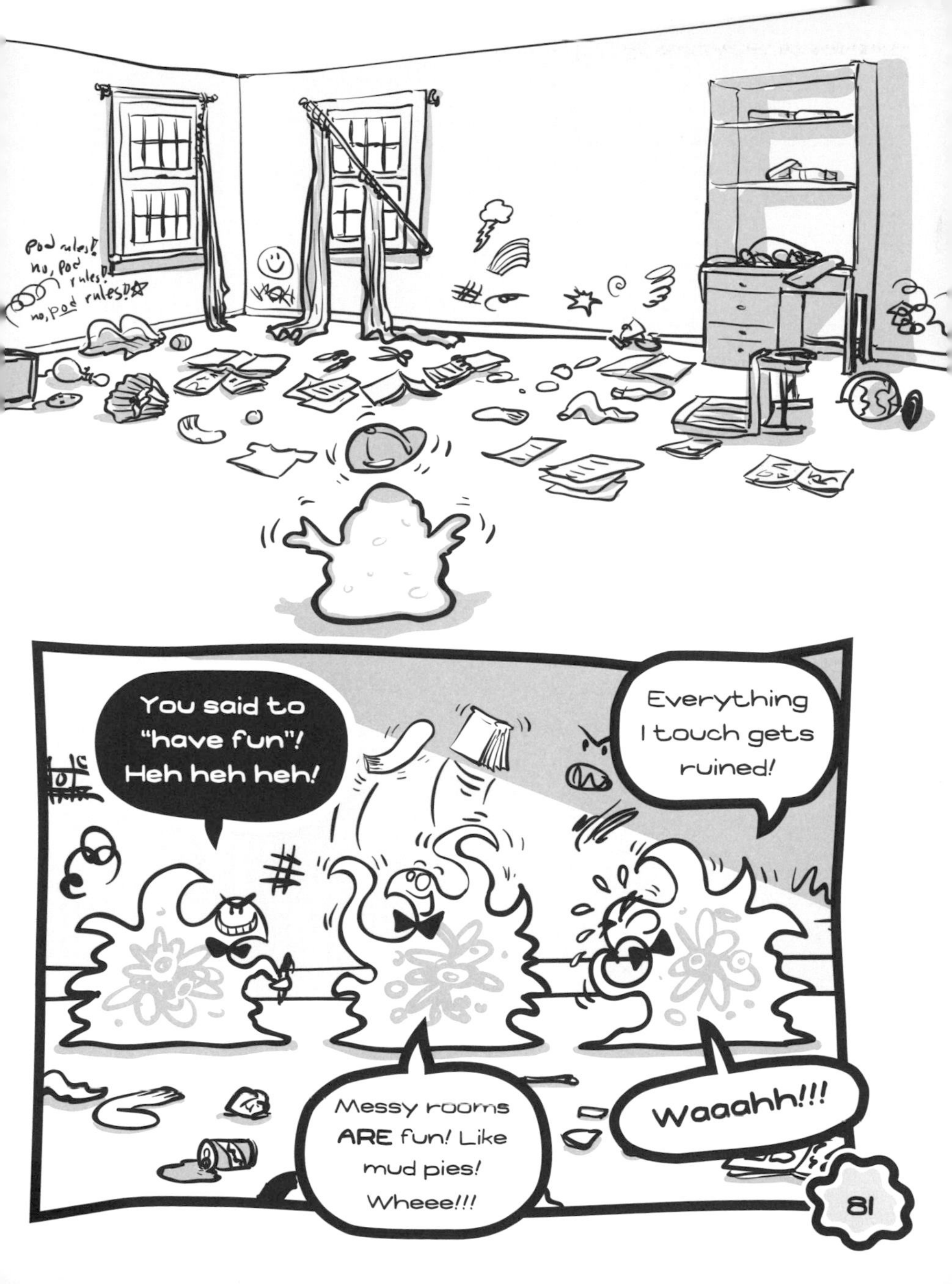

Pod rules!
no, Pod rules!
no, pod rules!
You said to "have fun"! Heh heh heh!
Everything I touch gets ruined!
Messy rooms **ARE** fun! Like mud pies! Wheee!!!
Waaahh!!!

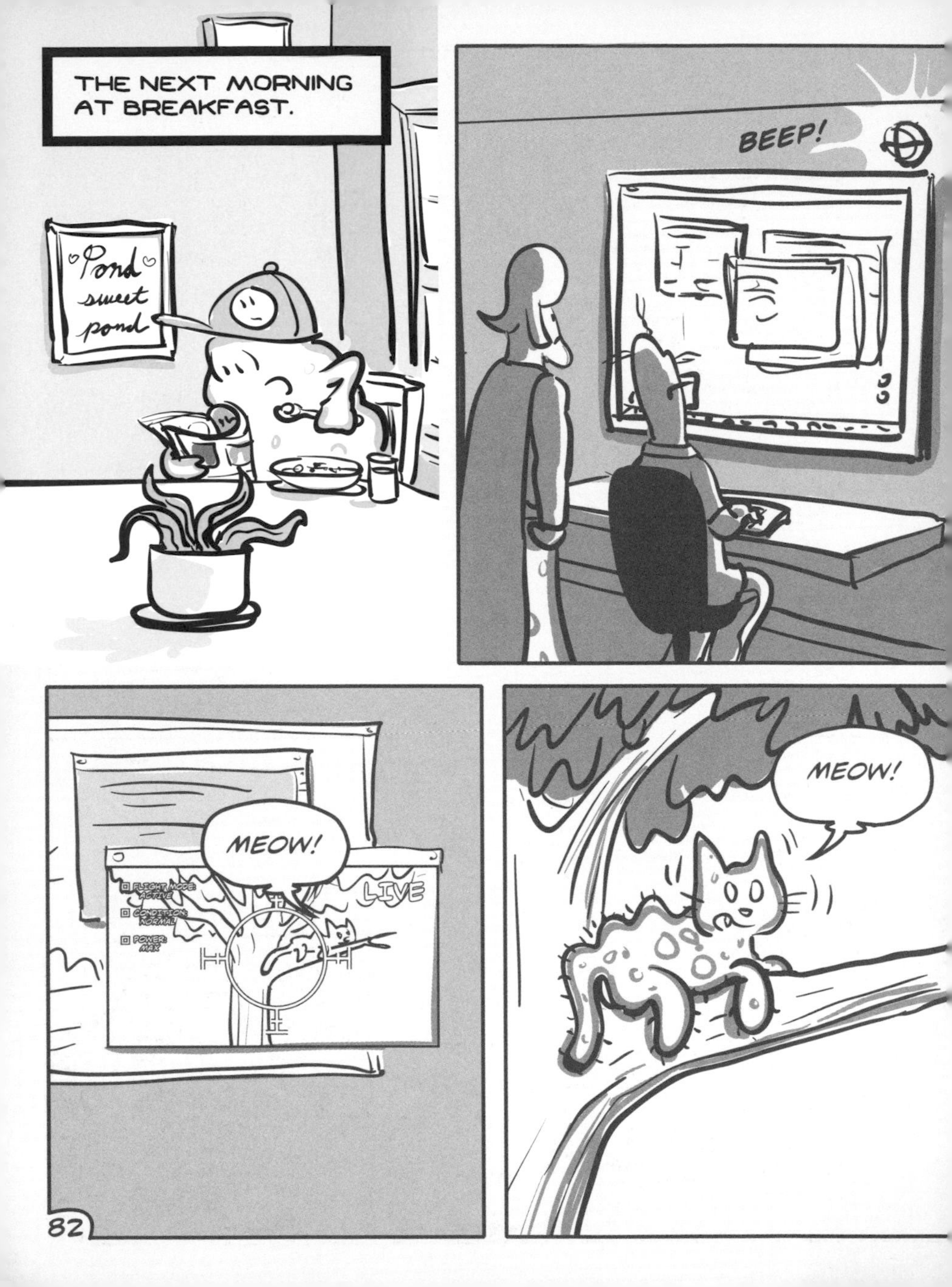
THE NEXT MORNING AT BREAKFAST.
Pond sweet pond
BEEP!
MEOW!
FLIGHT MODE: ACTIVE
CONDITION: NORMAL
POWER: MAX
LIVE
MEOW!

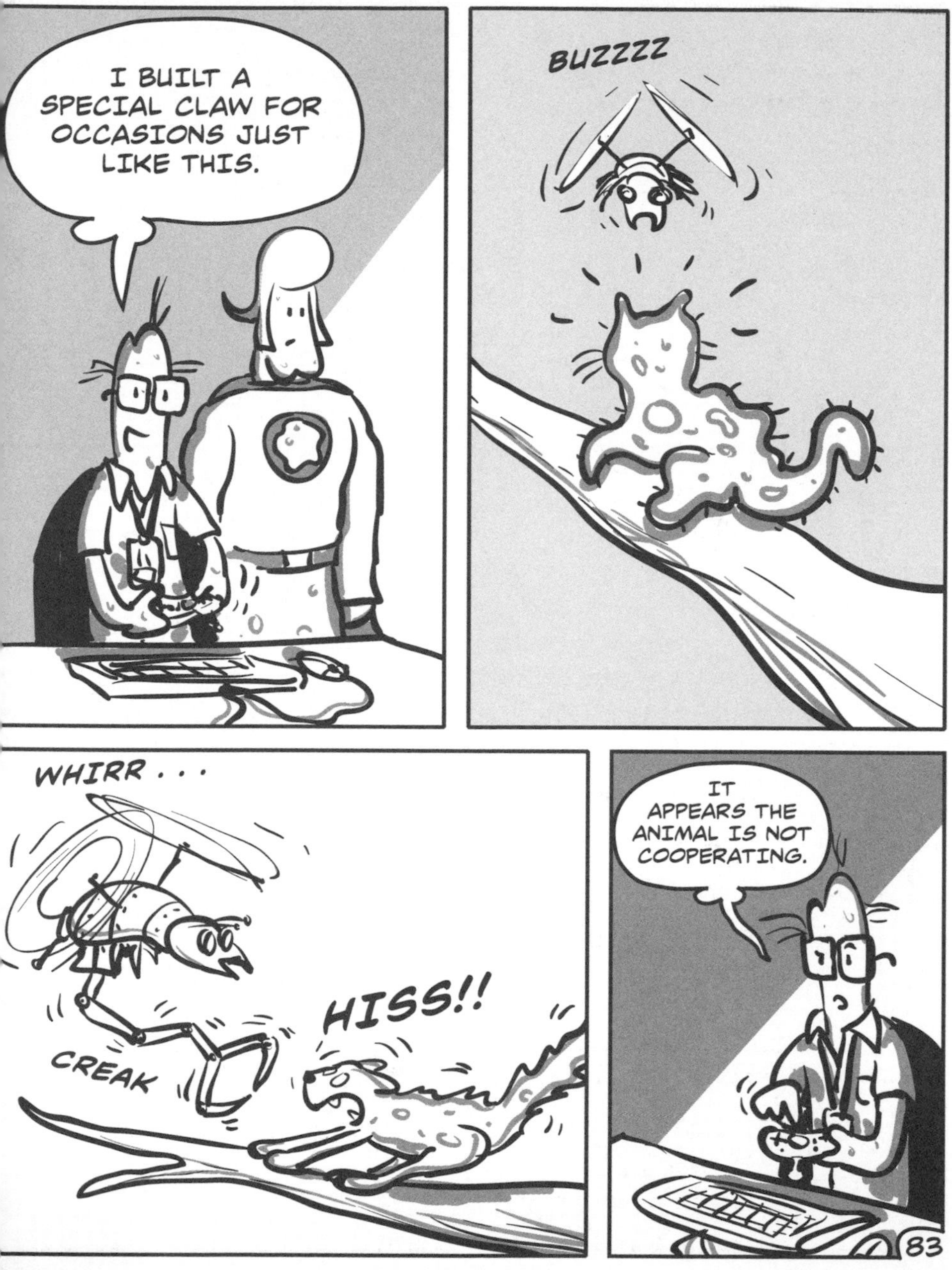
I BUILT A SPECIAL CLAW FOR OCCASIONS JUST LIKE THIS.
BUZZZZ
WHIRR . . .
CREAK
HISS!!
IT APPEARS THE ANIMAL IS NOT COOPERATING.

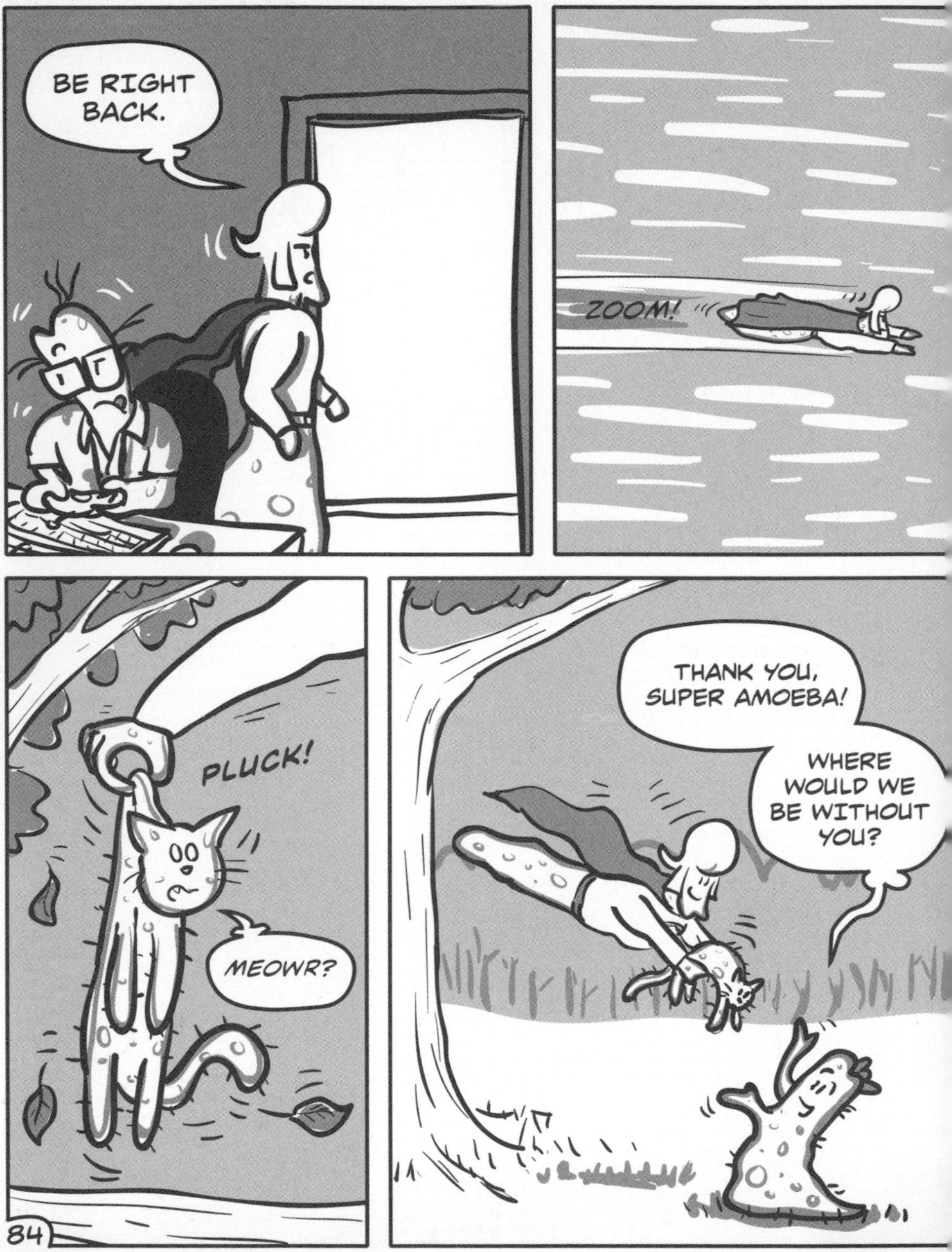
BE RIGHT BACK.
ZOOM!
PLUCK!
MEOWR?
THANK YOU, SUPER AMOEBA!
WHERE WOULD WE BE WITHOUT YOU?

SOMETIMES YOU HAVE TO DO THINGS THE OLD-FASHIONED WAY.
LATER.
YOU'RE SURE YOU DON'T WANT TO USE IT ANYMORE?
I PREFER THE WAY THINGS WERE BEFORE. IT MAY HAVE BEEN HARD, BUT IT WORKED FOR ME.
IT WAS NICE WORKING WITH YOU, S.A.!
AND YOU!
SHAKE
COME BY ANYTIME YOU WANT TO WATCH FUNNY CAT VIDEOS!

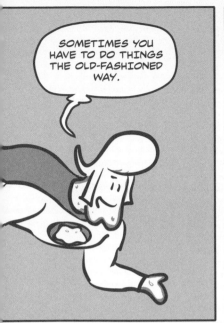

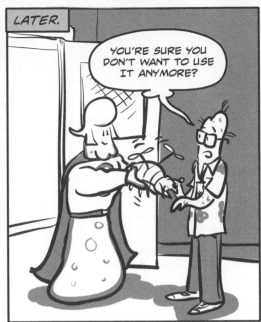

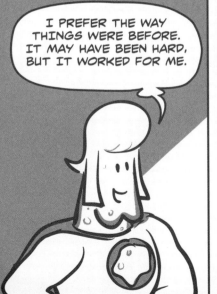

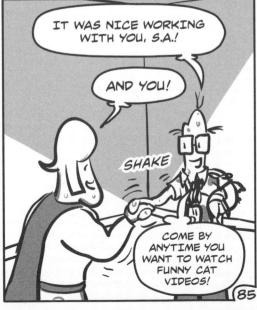

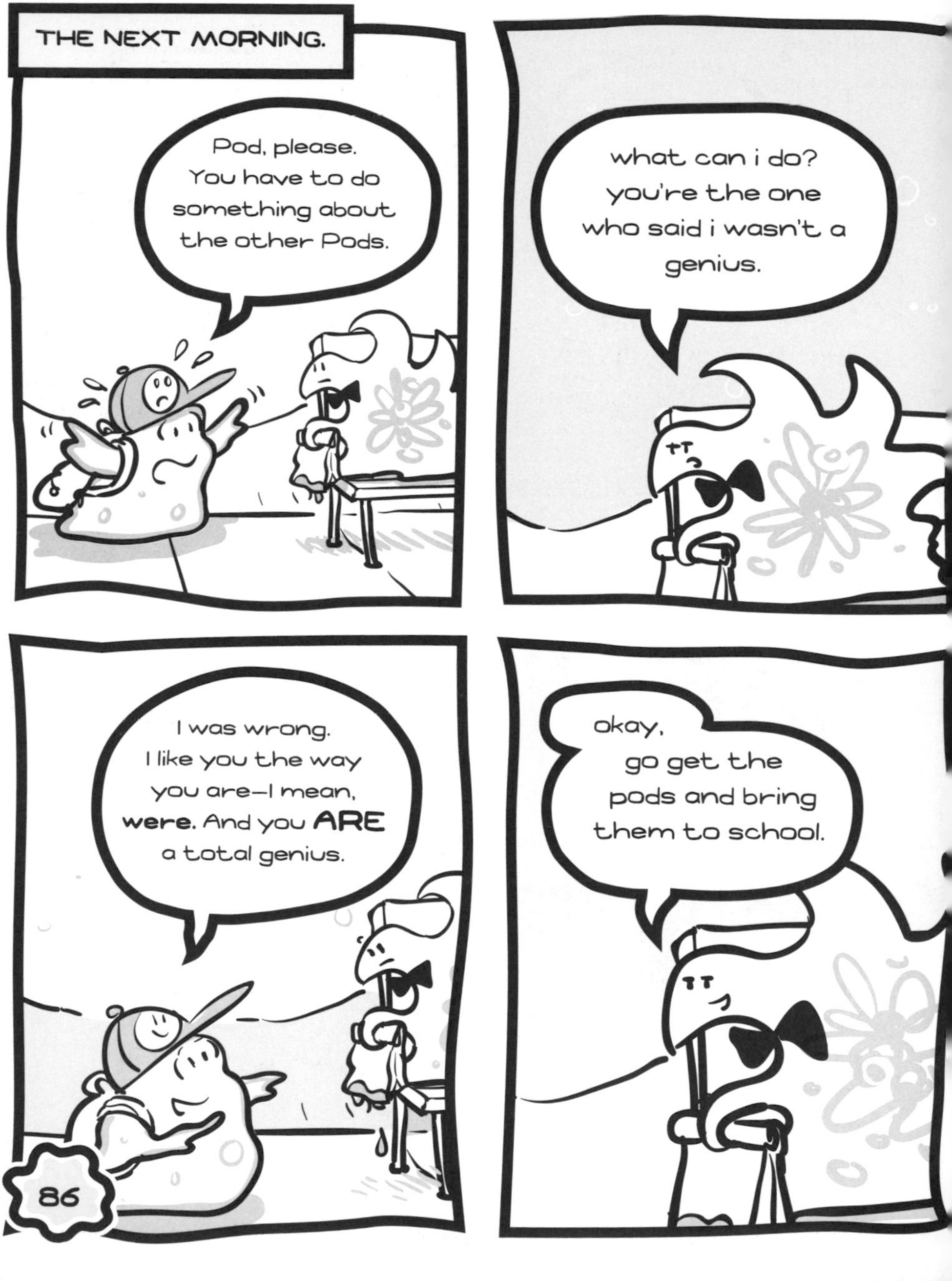
THE NEXT MORNING.
Pod, please. You have to do something about the other Pods.
what can i do? you're the one who said i wasn't a genius.
I was wrong. I like you the way you are—I mean, **were.** And you **ARE** a total genius.
okay, go get the pods and bring them to school.

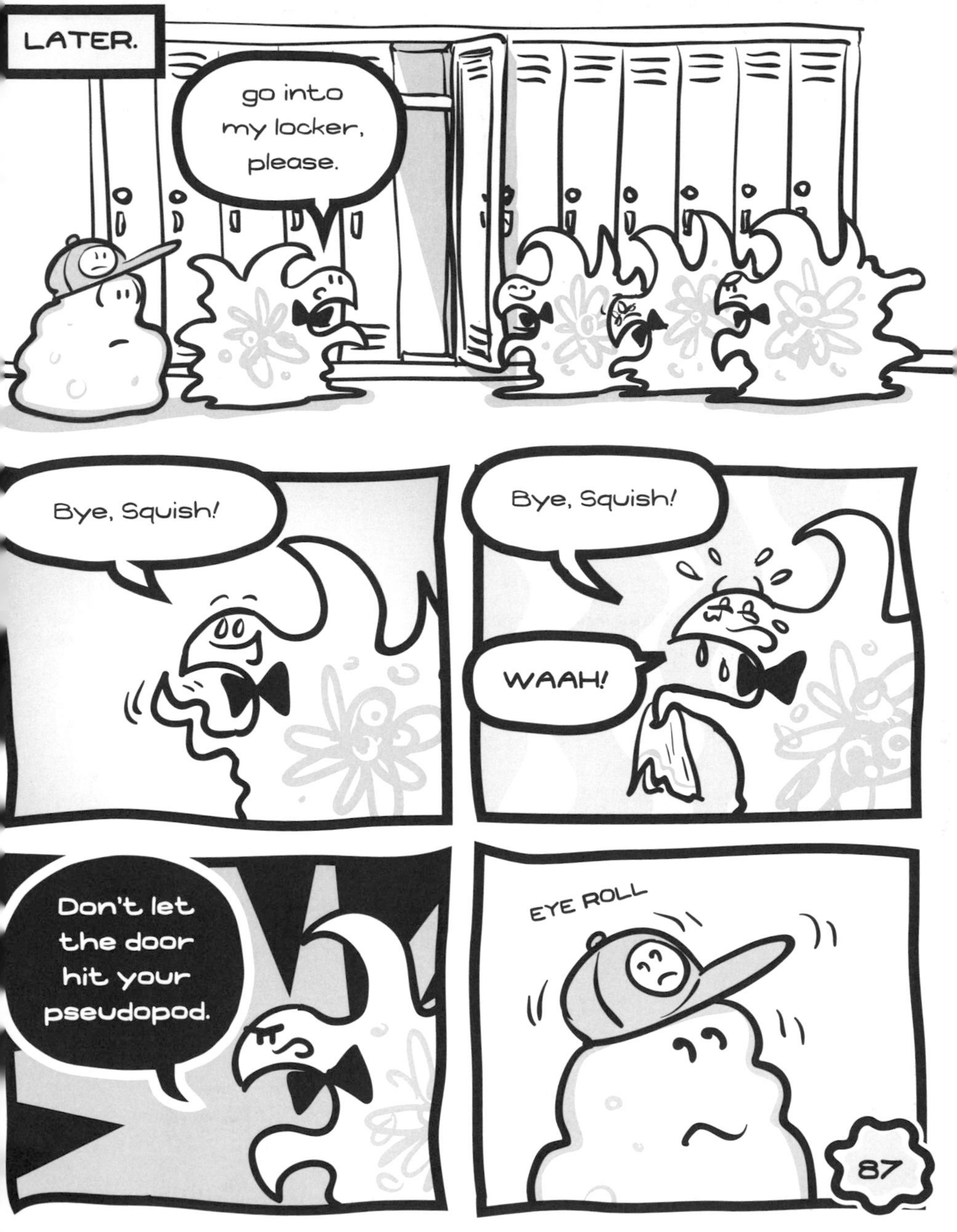
LATER.
go into my locker, please.
Bye, Squish!
Bye, Squish!
WAAH!
Don't let the door hit your pseudopod.
EYE ROLL

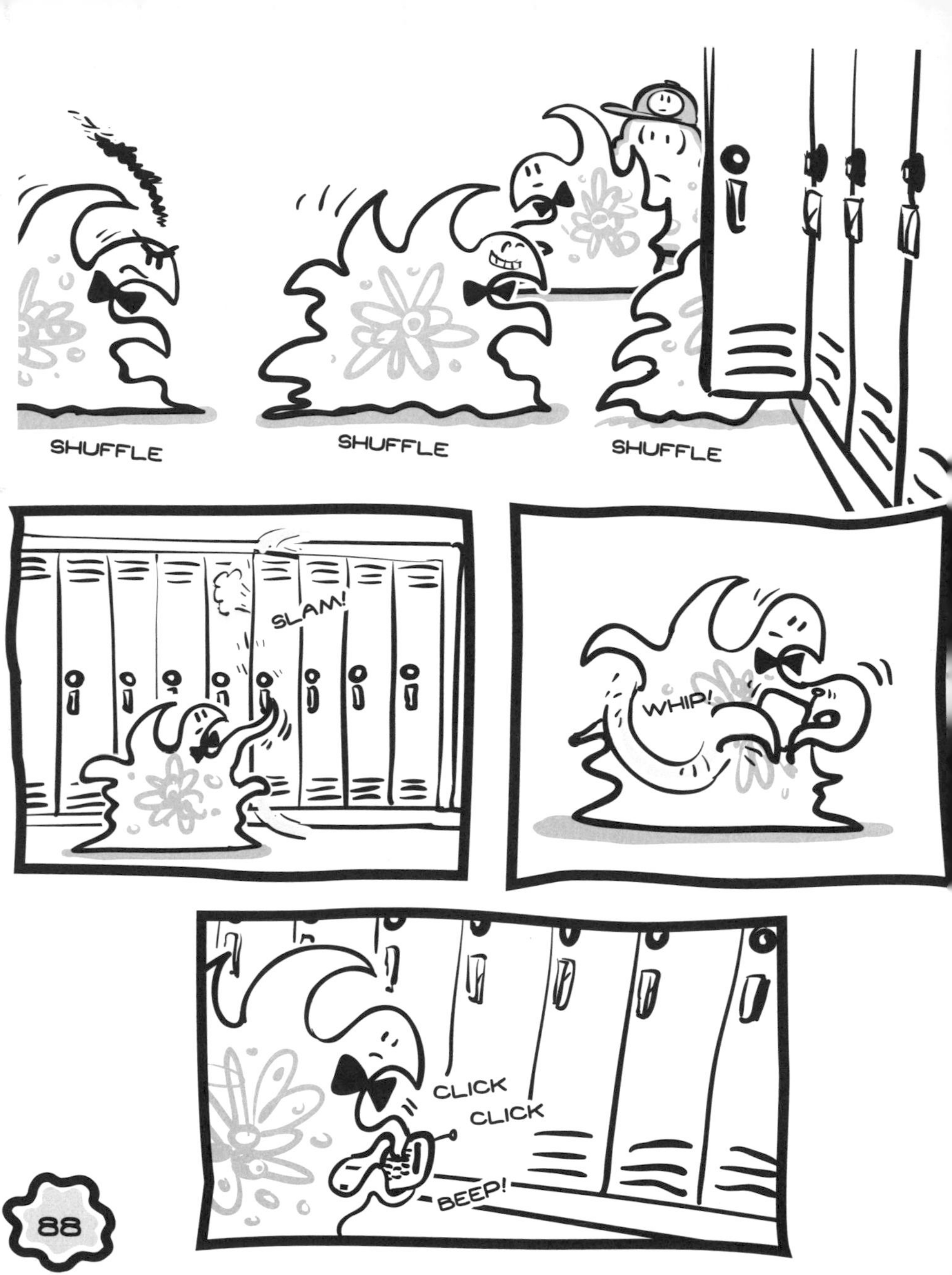
SHUFFLE
SHUFFLE
SHUFFLE
SLAM!
WHIP!
CLICK
CLICK
BEEP!

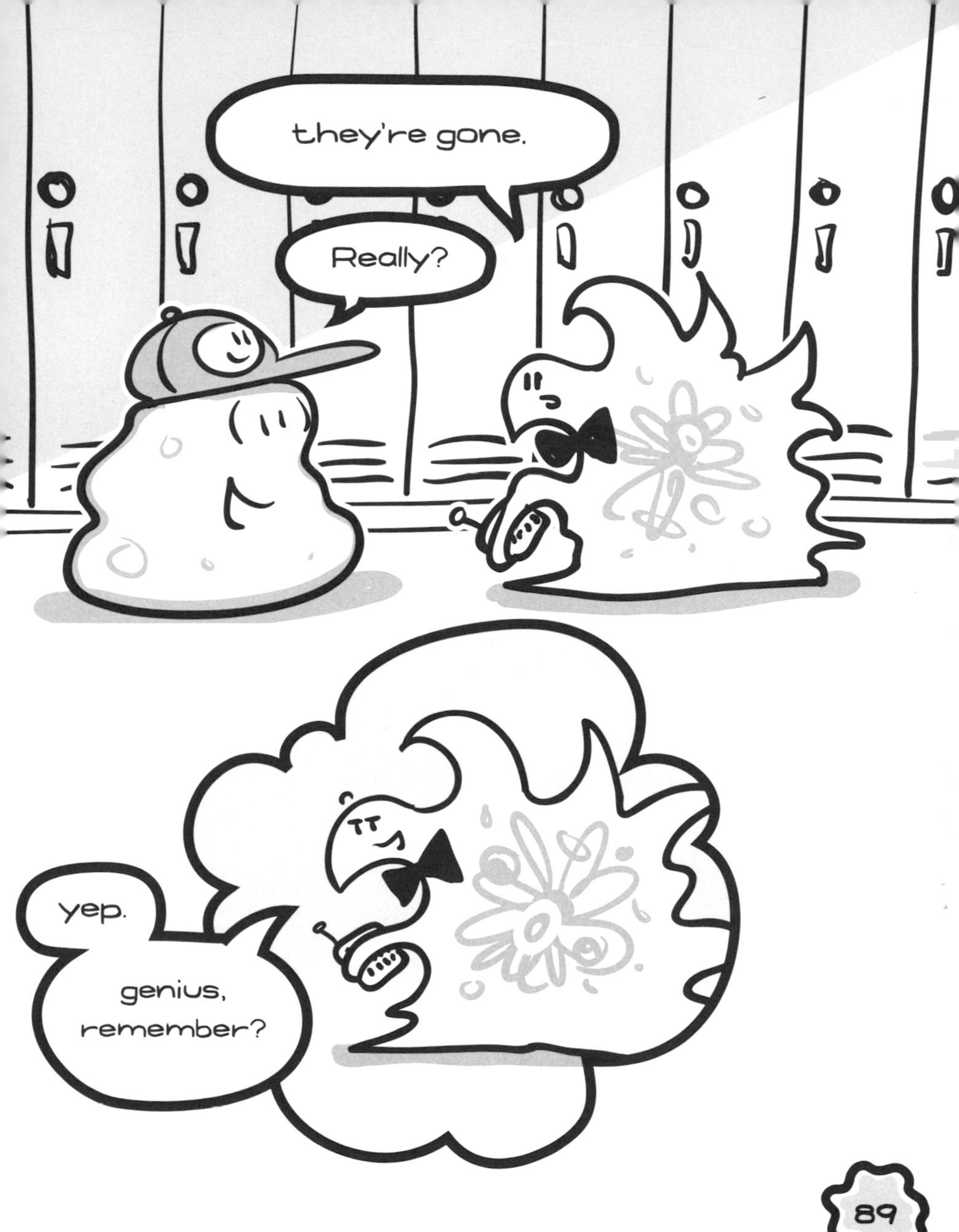
they're gone.
Really?
yep.
genius, remember?

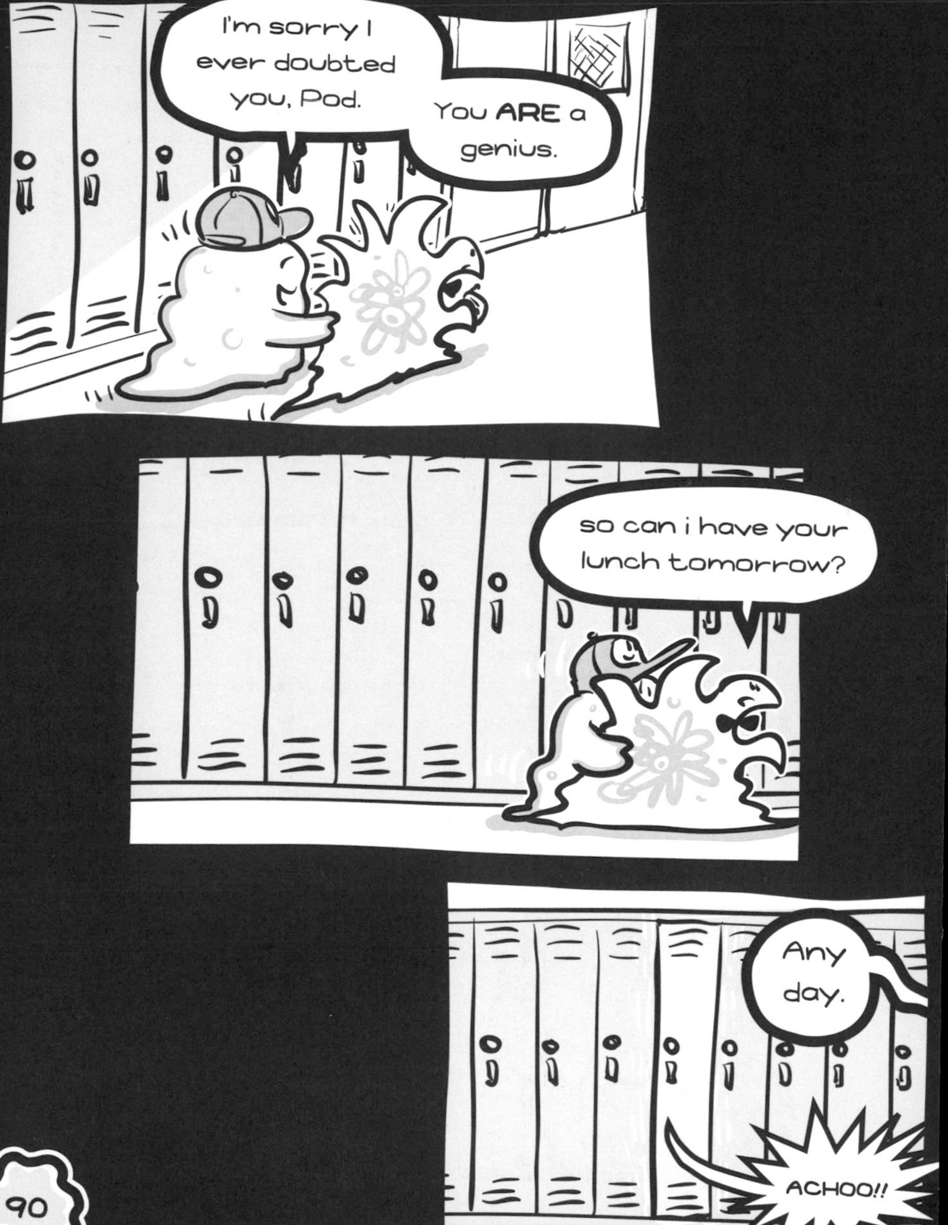
I'm sorry I ever doubted you, Pod.
You **ARE** a genius.
so can i have your lunch tomorrow?
Any day.
ACHOO!!

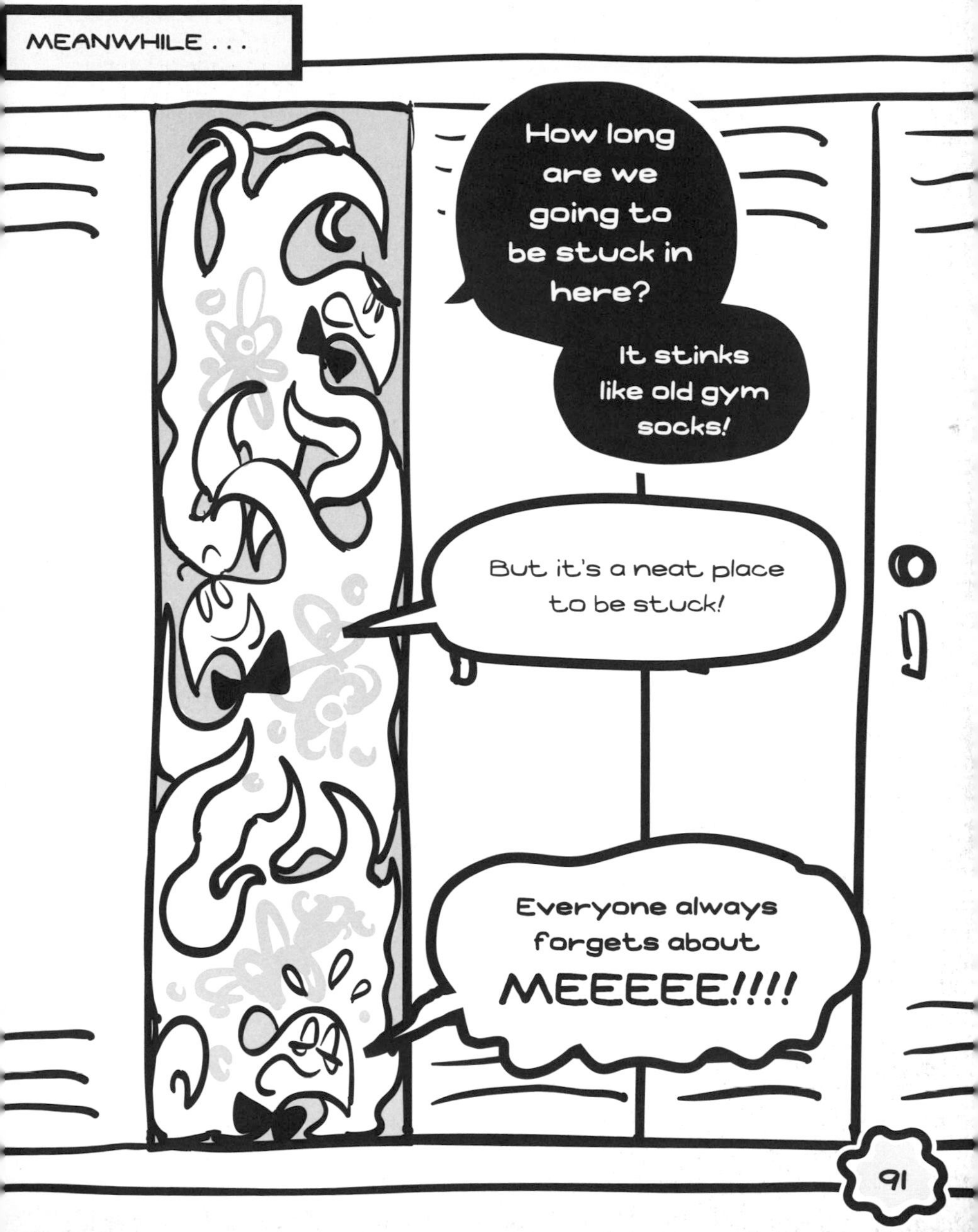
MEANWHILE . . .
How long are we going to be stuck in here?
It stinks like old gym socks!
But it's a neat place to be stuck!
Everyone always forgets about MEEEEE!!!!

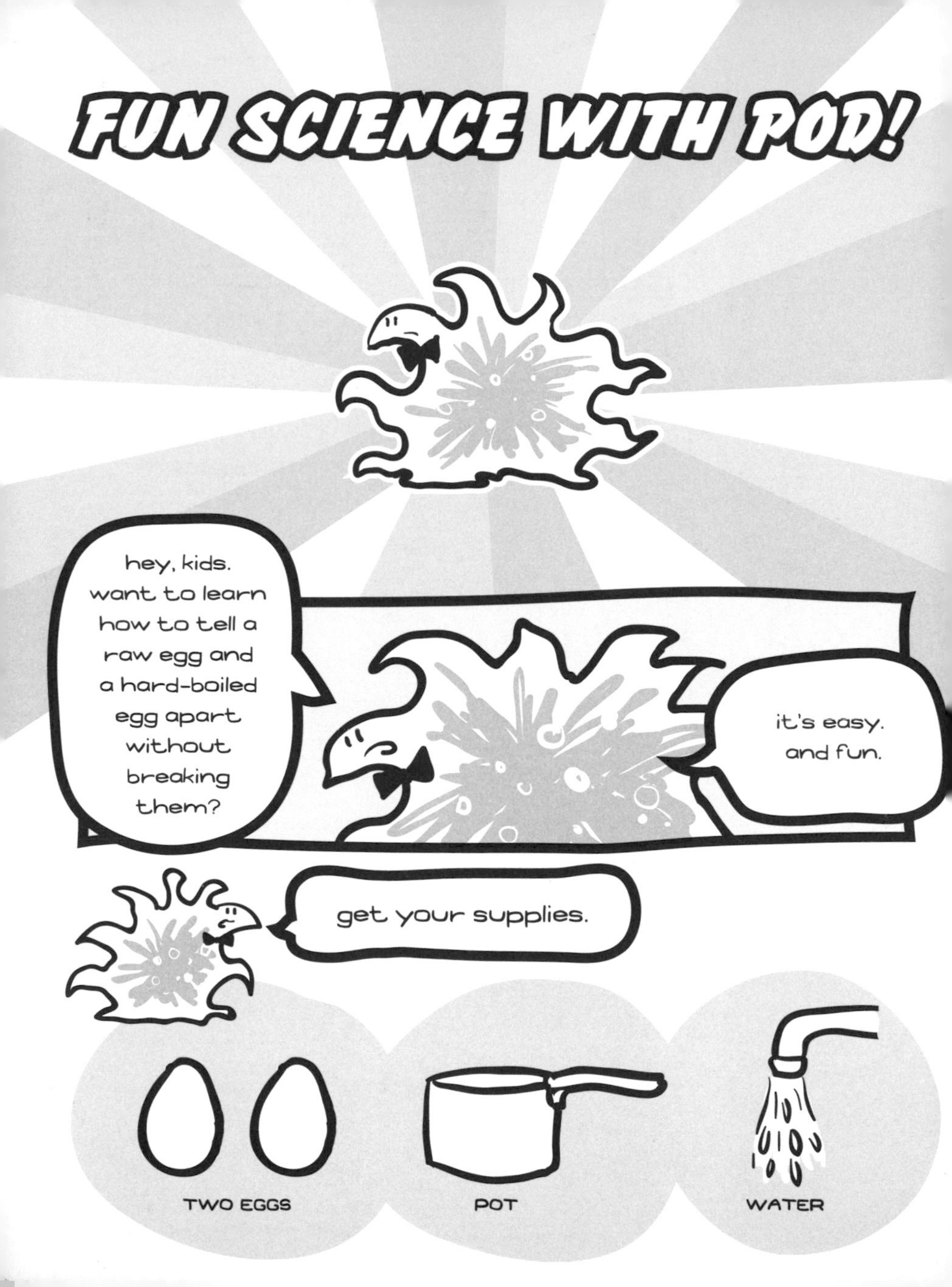
FUN SCIENCE WITH POD!
hey, kids. want to learn how to tell a raw egg and a hard-boiled egg apart without breaking them?
it's easy. and fun.
get your supplies.
TWO EGGS
POT
WATER

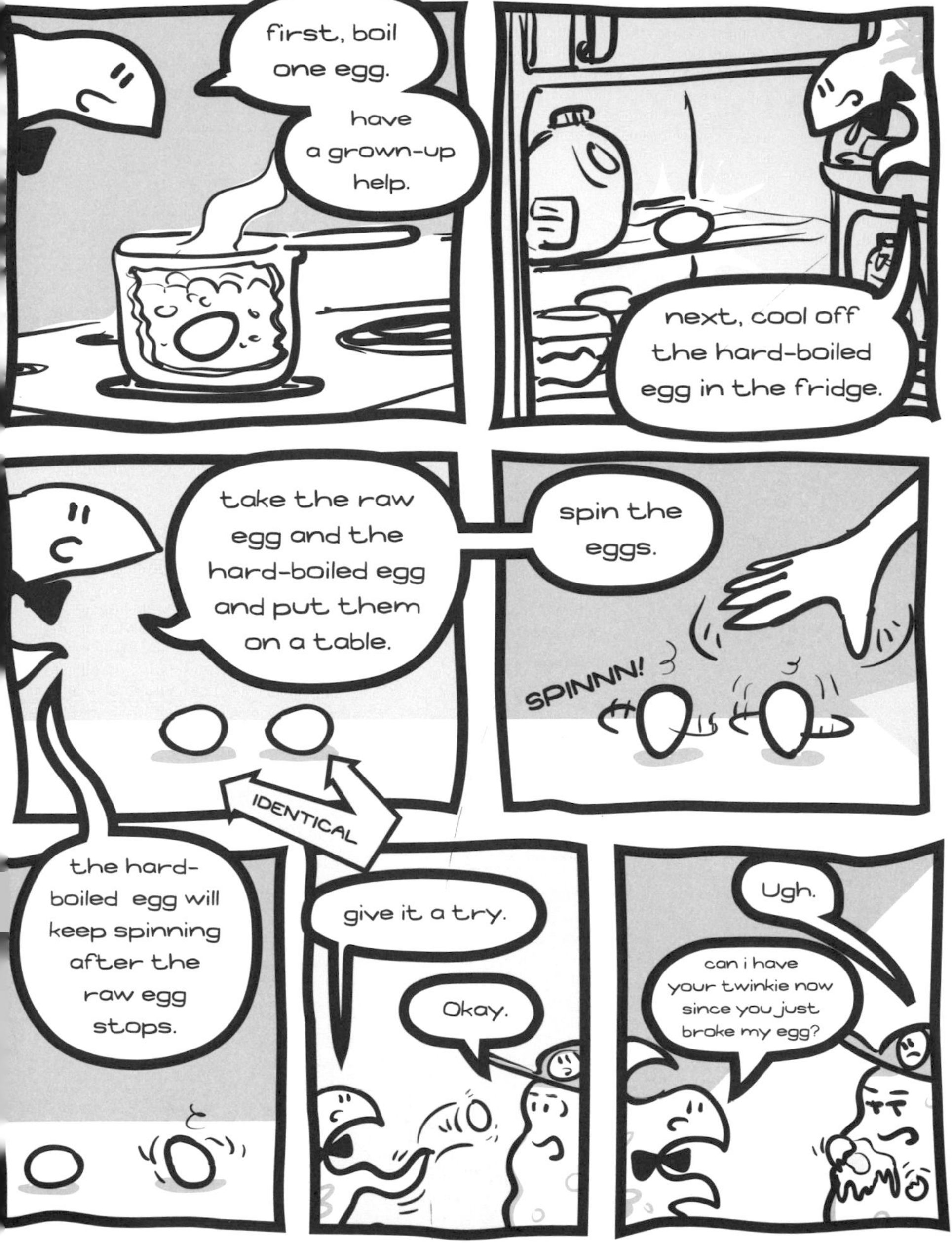
first, boil one egg.
have a grown-up help.
next, cool off the hard-boiled egg in the fridge.
take the raw egg and the hard-boiled egg and put them on a table.
spin the eggs.
SPINNN!
IDENTICAL
the hard-boiled egg will keep spinning after the raw egg stops.
give it a try.
Okay.
Ugh.
can i have your twinkie now since you just broke my egg?

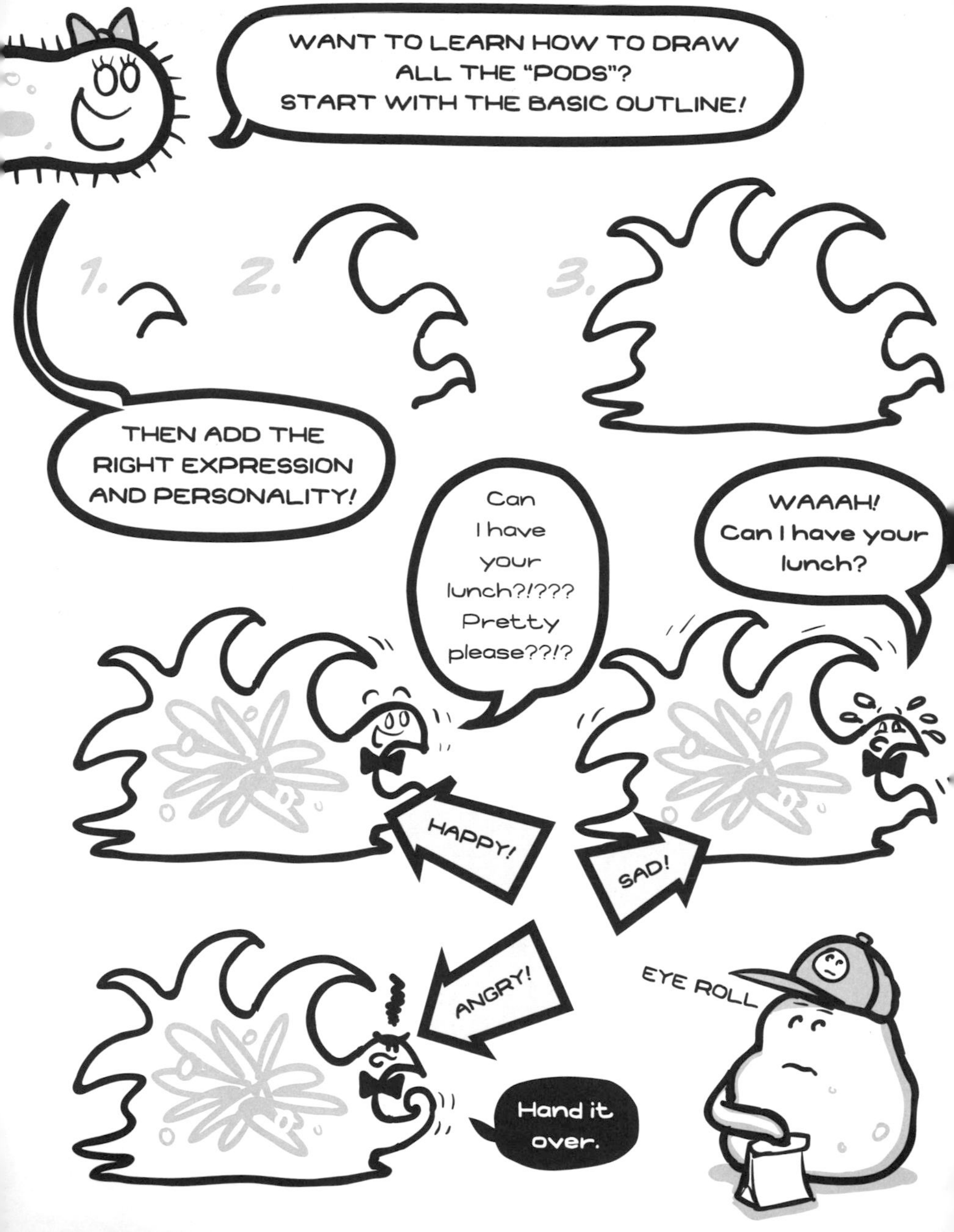

WANT TO LEARN HOW TO DRAW ALL THE "PODS"? START WITH THE BASIC OUTLINE!
1.
2.
3.
THEN ADD THE RIGHT EXPRESSION AND PERSONALITY!
Can I have your lunch?!??? Pretty please??!?
WAAAH! Can I have your lunch?
HAPPY!
SAD!
ANGRY!
EYE ROLL
Hand it over.

IF YOU LIKE SQUISH, YOU'LL LOVE BABYMOUSE!

#1 BABYMOUSE: Queen of the World!

#2 BABYMOUSE: Our Hero

#3 BABYMOUSE: Beach Babe

#4 BABYMOUSE: Rock Star

#5 BABYMOUSE: Heartbreaker

#6 CAMP BABYMOUSE

#7 BABYMOUSE: Skater Girl

#8 BABYMOUSE: Puppy Love

#9 BABYMOUSE: Monster Mash

#10 BABYMOUSE: The Musical

#11 BABYMOUSE: Dragonslayer

#12 BABYMOUSE: Burns Rubber

#13 BABYMOUSE: Cupcake Tycoon

#14 BABYMOUSE: Mad Scientist

#15 A Very BABYMOUSE Christmas

#16 BABYMOUSE for President

#17 Extreme BABYMOUSE

#18 Happy Birthday, BABYMOUSE!

#19 BABYMOUSE: Bad Babysitter

#20 BABYMOUSE Goes for the Gold

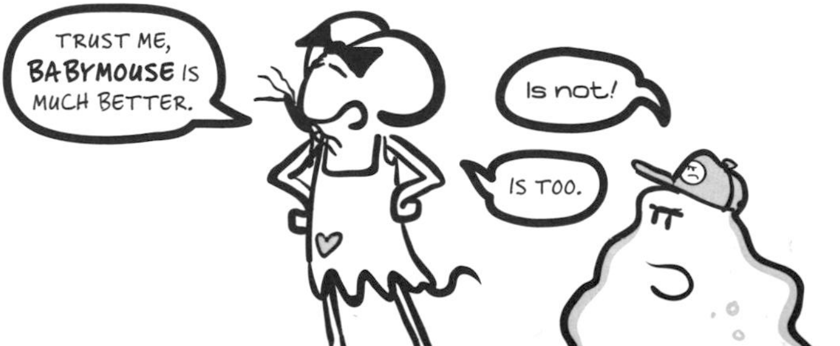
TRUST ME, BABYMOUSE IS MUCH BETTER.
Is not!
IS TOO.

DO YOU LIKE COMICS?
DO YOU LIKE LAUGHING TILL
MILK COMES OUT OF YOUR NOSE?

AVAILABLE NOW!